RETRIBUTION

THE MILLENNIUM GIRL (BOOK 2)

Stephen Westland

Also by the author

Mutation
The Millennium Girl Series Book 1
Stephen Westland
Copyright ©2014
All Rights Reserved

Retribution (2015)
The Millennium Girl Series Book 2
Stephen Westland
Copyright ©2015
All Rights Reserved

Transhuman (2015)
The Millennium Girl Series Book 3
Stephen Westland
Copyright ©2015
All Rights Reserved

The Envelope - A Collection of Very Short Stories (2014)
Stephen Westland and Helen Disley (editors)
Copyright ©2014
All Rights Reserved

Murderous Tales - A Collection of Very Short Stories (2014)
Stephen Westland and Helen Disley (editors)
Copyright ©2014
All Rights Reserved

AUTHOR'S NOTE

The author is grateful to Dian Li who designed the cover and to Helen Disley for proofreading the manuscript.

Contact Stephen Westland via email at
stephenwestland@gmx.com

Amelia Savage is a 17 year-old girl who is one of the lucky few that survived the great plague that wiped out ninety-nine per cent of the human population in 2022. Separated from her family she emerges from her bunker to find a world that is changed beyond her imaginings; a post-apocalyptic landscape dominated by a dystopian government elite and inhabited by brutal scavengers. Her mother is missing, her brother is killed, and her father is held captive. If you were her, wouldn't you want retribution?

The world would probably be a better place if we in developed countries worried a bit less about whether we will live to be 100, and a bit more about whether children born in the poorest countries will live to see their first birthday – *Stephen Cave, 2012* (from *Immortality: The Quest to Live Forever and How it Drives Civilization*)

RETRIBUTION

Contents

MUTATION

CHAPTER 1

CHAPTER 2

CHAPTER 3

CHAPTER 4

CHAPTER 5

CHAPTER 6

CHAPTER 7

CHAPTER 8

CHAPTER 9

CHAPTER 10

CHAPTER 11

CHAPTER 12

CHAPTER 13

CHAPTER 14

CHAPTER 15

CHAPTER 16

CHAPTER 17

CHAPTER 18

CHAPTER 19

CHAPTER 20

CHAPTER 21

CHAPTER 22

CHAPTER 23

CHAPTER 24

CHAPTER 25

CHAPTER 26

CHAPTER 27

CHAPTER 28

CHAPTER 29

CHAPTER 30

About the Author

Mutation

A Personal Message

MUTATION

Irrevocable change rocked the world in 2022 with the great plague that reduced a worldwide population of more than nine billion to one of less than eighty million in just over a year. Once infected, within a couple of days victims would develop a fever, headache and muscle pain. Their skin would break into an itchy rash with puss-filled boils and the victim would begin to feel tired and lethargic as severe flu-like aches and pains set in. Body temperature would rapidly increase and the victim would suffer vomiting and diarrhoea. Internal bleeding would occur about one week after infection in most cases and death would follow shortly afterwards. The rate at which the disease spread was brutal, accelerated by the extent of international travel and the free movement of people. What few knew at the time was that the virus was introduced intentionally to purge the earth from the humanpox that the elite thought the working masses had become. The Ebola virus had killed hundreds of thousands as it raged across the Earth in 2015; however, it could only be passed through intimate contact via body fluids. In the end it had been contained but not destroyed. Samples of the virus had been retained in secret laboratories and modified so that it could be transmitted by airborne particles. There it remained, waiting for the moment when it would be released.

The block was an underground secure government facility on the island of Anglesey off the coast of North Wales. Those who were invited to the block were the lucky ones but did not see it that way; they considered themselves to be worthy of being saved, not recipients of luck at all. In their eyes, they were saved because they were worth saving. Some thought that the government facilities were akin to the biblical ark. Except that the ark was ostensibly based on fair representation whereas places in the block were offered on the basis of power and wealth or, in the case of the scientists and engineers that were saved, because they were useful to the powerful and the wealthy. The scientists, politicians and oligarchs who possessed *golden tickets* were spared the horror of the virus that was released on the rest of the population. Whilst they enjoyed their secure isolation in the underground block, filtered air and independent power supplies providing a safe living environment, above them people were dying. Seventy thousand people had lived on the island of Anglesey but less than a year after the first case of death from the virus was recorded there were fewer than seven hundred of those people left. These seven hundred people, oblivious to the living facility below their feet, could have been forgiven for thinking that those who died from the virus were the unfortunate ones. The ones who survived quickly realised that surviving the virus was a mixed blessing; horrors lay ahead that had been truly unimaginable and that were incomparable to their previously sophisticated, warm and safe lives.

As society's infrastructure imploded food became scarce. People ate rats, people stole from, and killed, their neighbours for food, and eventually people ate people. Life was no longer about living; it was about surviving. The rules were simple – you ate what you killed. A year after the virus had started to wipe out humanity there were fewer than four hundred on Anglesey as starvation, murder, war and cannibalism, the latter a rare but undeniable fact, continued to deplete the population. But just as it seemed that some semblance of stability had been achieved the remaining inhabitants of Anglesey were subject to a further and harsh injustice.

Out of the bowels of the block the government military forces emerged. They were in good health, well conditioned and, above all, very well armed. Driving armoured vehicles and forming wide lines of infantry they swept in a south-easterly direction. The remaining residents of Anglesey were hounded across the two bridges that spanned the Menai Strait, the water between Anglesey and the mainland of North Wales. Those that didn't flee were slaughtered. The soldiers sprayed machine-gun fire in wide arcs and cut down women and children indiscriminately. Their orders were brutal; clear the island, secure the island, and burn the bodies. Three days after they had emerged, plumes of sickly black smoke rose from several places on the island where piles of bodies had been set on fire. It was later estimated that at least two hundred men, women, and children were murdered by the soldiers before the orders were deemed to have been carried out. By the time the non-military personnel emerged there was no sign of the carnage that had preceded them. The Millennium Bridge and the Menai Suspension Bridge, the only ways to access the island on foot, were guarded to keep the island secure and the dead bodies had been shovelled into pits, set on fire, and then covered with soil.

At the time of the outbreak Professor Jon Savage had been on the cusp of a new gene treatment that could extend the life of humans for up to a thousand years. He was unwilling to be part of the purge, as the release of the virus became known, and resisted the plan for the elite to live for hundreds of years whilst billions of innocent souls died in agony. Instead, he and his family had remained underground for twenty-five years in deep hibernation.

They awoke in 2047 to a world that was changed beyond belief. His daughter, Amelia Savage, would be the first person to live for one thousand years thanks to the gene treatment her father gifted to her.

Her first taste of the new world was Anglesey in North Wales where the government survivors dominated the remaining ordinary people who lived on the mainland, who they referred to as scavengers. Sophie Wassell, head of security at Anglesey, desperately sought Amelia's father and the knowledge that only he possessed; the power to effectively live forever. For it was thought that once human life was extended to a thousand years or more it would allow people to live until such time as death from old age or disease would effectively be eliminated. Humans would become immortal – transhuman. Professor Savage had been presumed dead, but once it became known that Savage was still alive, Amelia became a valuable bargaining chip that Sophie hoped to exploit.

Disgusted by the decadence of the people at Anglesey Amelia sought out the scavengers and discovered that they were not the monsters and cannibals that Sophie had led her to believe they were.

Led by the charismatic professor, the disparate groups of scavengers in North Wales cooperated to cross the bridges to the island and break the gates of Anglesey; they overthrew the government elite that had dominated the region for a quarter of a century and who had done their utmost to inhibit a return to civilisation for ordinary people. David Talbot, the president of Anglesey, and Sophie Wassell, his Head of Security, escaped the assault on their city and took Professor Savage with them as their captive.

CHAPTER 1

As Chloe scrambled over, she barely noticed that her feet almost disappeared in the mud and stagnant water on the other side of the stile. Her bare feet slipped as she started to push off and she fell forwards and had to break her fall with her hands, splashing into the water. She hurried to her feet and gave an anxious look backwards. There was no immediate sight or sound of her pursuer but that gave her no comfort at all.

The wooded area that she was making for was all that she was thinking about. In the open fields she knew that she had little chance to escape. In a straight race there was no possibility whatsoever that she could outrun her pursuer, or pursuers; there was at least one but she knew that they often travelled in pairs. There was every likelihood that two or more of them were on her tail.

Her heart was thumping and her lungs burned with the strain of working hard to provide the oxygen that her body demanded. She focussed hard on not falling and set her mind on reaching the next wooden gate on the other side of the field. All she could hear was her own heavy panting, resonating through her skull, as she sprinted across the rough grass. Twenty metres or so from the gate she looked back and saw that there were indeed two of them and that they had just cleared the style. She grunted with increased effort and raced forwards, hitting the wooden gate hard and scrambling up it. Her foot was on the top rung and she was just about to leap off when she heard a cracking sound, like wood being split by an axe, accompanied by an intense light that surrounded her. As it ignited beneath her, she realised that the gate had been hit by a laser. The horizontal wooden beams splintered and collapsed under her weight. She cried out as she fell forwards, landing in brackish shallow water, her arms unable to move quickly enough to cushion the fall.

Momentarily stunned, she somehow managed to get to her feet and keep moving. The edge of the forest was at the bottom of this field that sloped downwards for about eighty metres. If she could make the wooded area there was more chance that she could elude her assailants; the trees would give her cover and there was a chance that she would be able to move more swiftly than them between dense foliage. Breathing even more heavily now, and slowing, she started to feel a pain in her right calf and, as she became aware of it, it became intense. She paused, looked down and noticed that there was blood running down onto her foot. The laser must have struck her leg or else she had been injured as she fell from the gate. No matter how it had happened, there was a gash in the flesh of her calf just below the knee. Now that she was aware of her injury she was in a lot of pain and started to panic. She glanced backwards and saw her pursuers crashing through what remained of the wooden gate, charred pieces of wood flying to the sides as their powerful legs pumped forwards.

Chloe cried out, an involuntary call caused by her growing distress, and started to make for the wooded area that was almost within reaching distance now. However, the pain in her leg was growing and she was limping more than running. She screamed as her right leg gave way and she collapsed to the ground. For four or five seconds she was completely disoriented as she rolled down the gentle slope before coming to rest amongst stones and shrubs where the ground levelled off at the edge of the woods.

Groaning, she managed to get on to her hands and knees and as she looked up she saw one of her assailants was standing just ten feet away from her. She sensed movement to the left and noticed the other one was just arriving. It was over and she realised that she had only seconds left to live. She did not even consider pleading for her life, asking for pity. The thought never entered her head because she knew that the machines facing her had none. She thought she saw a red light, fractions of a second before lasers tore through her flesh and bones.

Amelia woke with a start, sweating and flushed, as she took several moments to realise where she was. It was already light in her room, sunlight streaming through the window and seagulls calling out from the rocks below. Erik was already up and she could hear him downstairs, preparing breakfast. It had just been a dream. She breathed out slowly, methodically, and let the sounds wash over her. She had no idea why she was dreaming about robots nor who the girl Chloe was.

CHAPTER 2

Erik studied the faded map, stretched out before them on the table, and smoothed his tanned hand over the surface of the aged paper.

"The centres in Oban and Petersfield are too far away. No way they could get there on a single charge. At a push if they had flown due south they may have made it to Dartmoor. Risky though."

"Kielder Water?" asked Amelia.

"Just within range ... I think. I made that journey twice before. Matlock would also have been within easy reach."

There were five known government centres, other than Anglesey. Erik was confident that Sophie Wassell, Head of Security for the now deposed Anglesey group, had fled with Amelia's father to one of these. It was inconceivable that they could have headed for anywhere else. Life outside of those centres was extremely hard and very dangerous.

Amelia was tall and muscular and had auburn hair that framed high, wide cheekbones and pale green eyes. A shapely body and athletic build gave little clue that she was possessed of immense strength; she could lift a two-hundred pound man effortlessly and throw him more than twenty metres away. Her strength stemmed from a genetic modification that had been gifted to her and her brother James by their father, John Savage, previously Professor of Human Genetics, currently held prisoner by Sophie Wassell. James had had no time to enjoy his newly endowed strength and longevity, nor even time to become aware of these attributes. He had been murdered, shot by one of Anglesey's city guards, the man that was currently sitting next to Amelia on the terrace of the refectory building in Anglesey and plotting how to locate and rescue her father.

"So what's your guess?" Amelia idly twirled her auburn hair around the index finger of her right hand as she studied the map of the British Isles that lay before her. "I would say Matlock, don't you think?"

Erik shook his head with his lips tightly pressed together before saying, "Talbot had a closer relationship with the group at Kielder Water than with any of the other groups. I have a feeling he has gone there. Besides, the helicopters flew out over the sea. If they had been heading for Matlock they would have headed for the south or the south-east at least."

Amelia was prepared to accept Erik's judgement. She knew that he had deep knowledge about the way in which Talbot and Wassell thought whereas she had only known Sophie Wassell for a matter of months and had barely met Talbot. Nevertheless, she had one further doubt. "Don't you think they could have gone north and then looped around to the south?"

"Why do you think they would do that?"

"Well, they didn't know we didn't have any RPGs on the mainland. Heading out to sea was the safest thing to do even if they had been intending to go south to Matlock eventually."

Erik nodded and dropped his gaze for a few moments. "Good point," he said. "I just think that they would've gone where they could be most certain of a warm welcome. I think that's Kielder Water. They would view it as a safe house." He paused for a few seconds before continuing. "Look, the bottom line is that we don't know ... but my instinct tells me Kielder Water."

"Well, we have to start somewhere," said Amelia, who had accepted Erik's instinct. "I'll go with your best guess."

David Talbot had been the President of Anglesey and had left the city by helicopter with Sophie Wassell and Jon Savage shortly before it surrendered to the overwhelming forces that had invaded from the mainland. As a senior member in the security team at Anglesey, Erik had accompanied Talbot and Wassell on occasional visits when they had been to some of the other government centres. Each of the six centres in the United Kingdom had populations comprising the elite; financial oligarchs and politicians from the old world who had been deemed important enough to be saved from the great purge, and their children, since twenty-five years had now passed since the world's population had been purged by the virus.

"So how do we get there?" said Amelia bluntly. She was all too aware that whichever centre they went to first they could be wrong. She had always thought that the best course of action in such circumstances was to go on instinct. Kielder felt right to Erik and that was good enough for her.

Not a day had passed by that she had not thought about her father. Apart from a moment on the roof of the administrative building in Anglesey, the day when her father was bundled into one of the two helicopters that fled the falling city, Amelia had not seen her father for more than a quarter of a century despite the fact that she was only seventeen years old; though for most of those twenty-five years she had been asleep in a state of suspended animation as she and her family avoided the terrors of the virus and the debilitating effects on society that unfolded above their secure bunker. She also missed her mother and there had been no news whatsoever about her fate. In many ways not knowing was worse than knowing bad news, but in the case of her father she at least had something to focus on, something to hold on to. She was therefore concentrating her efforts on finding Sophie Wassell. When she had gone to sleep in the pods, during the outbreak of the virus, she had been a normal teenage girl. Now, almost everything she knew had been ripped away. In addition to her friends, her culture and her environment, all of which were gone, her brother had been killed, her mother had vanished and was presumed dead, and her father was being held captive by someone that Amelia could only describe as a maniac. Those things that had been ripped away were not coming back but at least in the case of her father there was a potential recovery.

Two months had elapsed since the fall of Anglesey, during which time the city had started to be rebuilt and a new administration had been put into place to run the city and its surrounds. Many of the scavengers who had taken part in the assault decided to stay there to rebuild the city and sent for their families to join them. Others returned to their homes at places like Conway, where the castle, a safe and secure store house, was renovated to recapture some of its long-lost splendour as a formidable fortification. Now that the threat of capture or death from the helicopter raids from Anglesey had been removed, the land around Conway was put to its proper use for large-scale farming. For the first time in decades, many people felt optimistic about the future; or, at least, they had increased confidence that they had a future. People started to plan and organised themselves in a way that they did not consider before, when survival was the main focus.

Despite the fact that Erik had been their enemy before the fall of Anglesey he was asked to remain in his role with the City Guard by the new hierarchy. In part, this was due to the fact that Peter Carr, the ex-soldier who had assumed command directly after the city surrendered, had argued that if they were to succeed going forward they needed to work together no matter what had happened in the past. It was also partly because of Erik's closeness to Amelia who, as the daughter of the man who had planned the assault on the city and persuaded the various groups in North Wales to join him, had a special status amongst the scavengers. Any lingering doubts about where Erik's loyalty lay were quickly dissipated when stories emerged about his role in saving Amelia's life after Sophie had ordered her to be killed. He had risked his own life to save Amelia's.

Since that fateful day Amelia and Erik had become lovers. Erik had saved Amelia's life on at least two occasions but he had also killed her brother and deceived her when he knew that her brother was dead even as he pretended to help her look for him. Despite this, Amelia trusted him. It was hard to explain why, but perhaps the intense experiences they had shared after their helicopter had been shot down had acted as a catalyst for the bond that now existed between them. Perhaps it was in part because she had nobody else to turn to. It also helped that he was attractive, a

18

tall handsome man in his thirties, with thick dark hair and a wide mouth. When he spoke his voice was soothing and controlled but naturally authoritative when the situation demanded it.

He looked at her with his deep olive-brown eyes set beneath dark eyebrows. "We have several helicopters here but the charge will only allow a one-way trip," he said.

Amelia nodded to indicate that she understood. She knew that the electrically powered helicopters were invaluable. There was a supply of spare parts but building new helicopters was impossible and the city needed to preserve the few that they had for as long as possible.

"However, I have another idea," Erik said, a smile lighting up his face, "but it won't be without risk."

Amelia returned the smile with a wide grin of her own. "Bring it on," she said, and leant forward kissing him full on the lips. She took his hand and led him off the terrace and towards their living quarters.

CHAPTER 3

Erik held Amelia's hand as the helicopter began its descent against a grey sky just south of Scotland's west coast near a town called Gretna. The plan was to take a route that shadowed a stretch of water that marked the border between England and Scotland, albeit a mile or so south of it, in a north-easterly direction to the Northumberland National Park district where the Kielder Water facility was located.

The helicopter had barely touched the ground before Erik jumped out and almost dragged Amelia down with him. They strode away from the craft with their backs bent over to avoid the still-spinning blades before Erik turned and gave the thumbs-up sign to the pilot who then swiftly ascended. The plan to land on the west coast was certainly not without danger. The helicopter would no doubt be seen by local inhabitants – Carlisle was only about four miles to the south – and would undoubtedly attract attention that may or not be hostile but would certainly be unwelcome. Amelia and Erik wasted no time and hurried away from the sandy shore to quickly put as much distance between them and the touchdown point as possible. Within a minute they were running across long grass and Erik looked back briefly to see the helicopter disappearing into the gloomy sky.

It was about fifty miles from here to their destination and Erik estimated that they could make this journey in three days. They had sufficient food and some water but proximity to clean drinking water had been a major consideration when planning their route. That was why they were staying close to the Liddel Water. The water could also potentially provide food should the trek take much longer than they expected. Of course, staying near to fresh water also had its risks.

Amelia thought back to the time when they had fought their way back from Manchester to Anglesey after their transport had been shot down whilst searching for her brother. On that occasion they had been unprepared – it had been a shock, like the feeling of jumping into icy water on a summer's day – whereas now they were ready for what was likely to be a three- or four-day slog across a barren countryside that would offer little sustenance to them and would most likely bring them into contact with people. Since that earlier adventure, Amelia had received training from Erik in the art of combat and this, along with her extraordinary strength, speed and rapid healing powers, made her a formidable combatant. Erik was also an experienced fighter but they were still only two and it was unlikely that they could fight their way across the land to Northumberland by force alone; stealth was the preferred option.

They jogged for nearly an hour in an easterly direction until they reached a motorway. Making their way down a grassy slope, the grey and empty concrete road curved away from them, both to the north and the south, like a dead snake. Once on the concrete – cracked and broken with weeds pushing through in several places – they took advantage of the cover provided by the high banks either side of the road to take a drink. Erik was sweating profusely and breathing heavily but Amelia was less tired as she squirted water into her mouth.

"You're fit," he said, panting and bent over double with his hands on his knees.

Amelia simply smiled. They both knew that her fitness was unnatural, one of the beneficial side effects of the gene treatment that she had received.

It was a few minutes before Erik was able to stand upright, even then still blowing heavily with his hands behind his head, stretching to fill his lungs with oxygen.

"So far so good?" he shouted up to Amelia who was now standing close to the top of the slope they had just descended which afforded her a good view over the fields from which they had come.

"Well, it looks as though nobody followed us," she said, scanning the horizon looking for any movement. There was smoke in the distance, far away to the south, but no sign that they had been tracked. It seemed that their strategy to move quickly away from the landing site had been effective. "At least, I can't see anyone." She turned back and scrambled back down to the road. "You ready?"

Erik took one last swig of water before slipping the silvery container into a pouch on the side of his bag. "Yep, that's a good idea."

They crossed the road and Amelia grinned as she found herself instinctively checking for traffic on the motorway before she realised what she was doing. Clambering up the bank on the other side, she reached the top first and held out her hand to help Erik up the last few yards. He grasped her hand firmly, knowing that she had more than enough strength to support him, and pulled himself to the summit.

"Thanks," he said.

There was a short silence as they looked across at the fields that lay just below them before Amelia asked, "Erik, you never mentioned any family back at Anglesey. You must have been, what, about ten when the virus hit?"

Erik nodded and made a small grunting sound which Amelia took as affirmation.

"You must have had parents when you entered the block. I'm guessing it was through them that you had your place."

"That's right," he said. "My father was Prime Minister for Wales."

It took a second or so for this to sink in. "Oh. Saunders. That's right, Gareth Saunders. That was the name wasn't it?" Amelia had known Erik's surname but had never thought to connect it with the Welsh Premier. "I remember him. He was pushing hard for full Welsh independence wasn't he?"

"Yep."

"So you came in with your parents. Any brothers or sisters?"

"I had a younger sister."

22

Amelia picked up straight away on the word *had*. "Do you want to talk about her?"

"No."

"What about your mum and dad? Are they still alive?"

"No. My father was Head at Anglesey when the block was first set up. He developed pneumonia a couple of years after we emerged from the underground and there were complications. That was when Talbot took over."

"Sorry to hear that."

"It's ok. It was ironic that a virus killed him, I guess. All that planning to escape the big one ..."

Amelia did not say anything straight away. She would never had guessed that Erik's father had been Talbot's predecessor. But now it made sense, with Erik having one of the most coveted jobs in Anglesey, though one that had admittedly not been without danger. Lots of things fitted into place now that she knew that Eric's family had been well connected. Only high-ranking officials had been allowed to bring their children with them to the blocks.

"And your mum?" said Amelia.

"She died just a couple of years ago. Cancer."

"Oh. Sorry."

Erik said nothing more and Amelia did not know what else she could say. They continued on in silence, noisily skidding down a gravelly slope, before trudging across an uneven field of knee-high washed-out green grass. A cool breeze blew dark clouds towards them, threatening rain.

CHAPTER 4

They walked briskly for about an hour until they came to a road. Erik checked his map, rotating it as he squinted at the sky and the glow of the sun that could be just discerned as a lighter grey area in the sky, and figured out that it was the one marked on the map as the A7. If they followed it north he knew that they would reach the place marked as Longtown but they agreed that such a course would be unwise. Longtown had been a small town with a population of about three thousand before the virus and would likely still be occupied. However, they did stay on the road for another hour or so because it was easy to walk along. So far, they had not seen a single person or, indeed, any evidence of any living people, but they did not allow this to let them become complacent. They walked for most of the time in silence and were constantly listening for any sounds that could indicate other people.

The road was flanked on either side with fields, segregated with low hedgerows in the style that was very typical of northern England. Eventually it led them to a more densely wooded area and Erik indicated that they should turn off the road here.

"We'll take a right here, Amy."

"Why here?" asked Amelia.

"We're getting close to the town. It's too risky to continue along the main road. Besides, this track will take us further east towards the Northumberland woods."

"How much longer are we going to keep going today? Even I could do with a break."

"I think we'll stop when we find a suitable place to sleep for the night. Don't know about you, but I need something to eat never mind a rest. We don't want to be getting there on our last legs, and another day won't make any difference."

Amelia shrugged. Another day probably would not make any difference. But on the other hand, it might. They had no way of knowing if her father was going to be at Kielder nor even if he would still be alive when they got there. As she walked along she could not help going through various scenarios in her head. She imagined arriving at Kielder and confronting Sophie. It was something she was looking forward to.

"Who are you talking to?" said Erik. He had seen her mouth engaged in silent conversation and her hands moving, as if expressing ideas, deep in conversation.

"Nobody," she replied, and then added, "Well, I was just imagining what I would say to Sophie when we get there."

"I thought it was something like that. But remember, getting your dad back is the main aim."

"I know. Don't you think I know that?"

Erik put his arm around Amelia's shoulder and gave her a hug. "I didn't mean to upset you." He kissed her head. "I know that's what you want. And I'll do everything I can to help you. But the plan is to get your father out. Sophie can wait until another day when he is safe."

Amelia gave a wry smile and responded to Erik's hug with one of her own.

They walked down a side road and came to a barn made of corrugated iron, with patches of brown and grey. The sides were heavily rusted and there were holes in some parts where the metal had been corroded away by time. However, the basic structure was still intact and the roof was still present. It would provide a good place to sleep. They approached the large shed cautiously and peered in through some of the holes to convince themselves that it was not occupied. Inside, the floor was filthy and scattered with assorted scraps of wood, plastic, metal and other materials; remnants of an earlier society. However, there were no obvious signs that the place was being occupied and that was important. Erik found some wooden pallets that were in reasonable shape and dragged them together to provide an area upon which they could sleep. They had brought light sleeping bags in their back packs and given that it was still late summer they would be warm enough to sleep here. The barn would protect them from the worst of the weather even if it were to rain. They enjoyed a simple meal of fruit, high-energy supplement, and water, whilst all the time listening carefully for any noises and watching the sky darkening through one side of the barn that was almost entirely open to the elements.

Amelia slept first and managed to drift off quickly but then slept fitfully, haunted by several dreams about her mother. She had not seen her mother since the day she had disappeared from the bunker. On that day her mother had gone up top to check whether it was safe. Amelia regretted that they had not gone together but her mother had insisted that she go alone and that Amelia and James stay safe in the bunker. Her dreams played around these events, over and over again, always in a different order but always with the same unpleasant outcome.

The sun was setting and Erik kept watch whilst Amelia slept in her bag, twitching from time to time, mumbling and moaning softly. The sound of Amelia's unquiet slumbers occasionally punctuated the background scratching noise of rats coming from the back of the barn. High up in the trees outside, a pair of owls hooted, clearly not too far away.

Amelia woke as she felt a hand on her mouth and someone shaking her shoulder. She quickly realised it was Erik and he kept his hand clasped over her lips as he put his other hand up to his own lips, making a signal to be quiet. Amelia understood immediately and got out of her sleeping bag quickly, but quietly, before following Erik over to the wall of the barn from where they could peer through to the road outside.

Strolling down the road, silhouetted against the dim grey light of the night that was enveloping the barn, they could see a group of scavengers. There were eight of them, six men and two women, and they chatted to each other as they walked, seemingly oblivious to the fact that they were being observed. Several of them carried bows with a quiver of arrows slung over their shoulders. Three dogs, border collies, walked with them, slipping between the gaps in their legs, as the group moved forward.

The dogs began to bark and the group stopped and looked around them. There was evidently some discussion. Erik and Amelia remained hidden and observed the group through two small gaps in the rusty metal wall. The dogs were sniffing the air and some of the men were looking towards the barn and pointing. Erik pulled out his semi-automatic firearm and watched the group closely, his fingers caressing the cold metal of the gun. He would rather avoid a fight if at all possible but felt reasonably confident that his superior firepower could take out the majority of the group before they had time to fire many arrows should it become necessary. As far as he could see they were not carrying any firearms although he knew that he could not rule out that they were. Amelia was carrying a semi-automatic handgun; it was a much smaller weapon than Erik's but lethal nonetheless and she was trained in its use. It was as if the leader of the group decided that there was nothing of interest here. Perhaps he thought that the dogs were excited by the distinctive sound and smell of rats, and he called on the others to keep going. Erik relaxed his grip and Amelia put her gun back into the holster that she wore around her hips. The holster reminded her of that fateful day that she and her brother James had emerged from their underground shelter after more than a quarter of a century. James had carried his father's gun in a holster much like the one Amelia was now wearing. Had he not taken the weapon with him it was possible that he would still be alive now; as it was, James had been killed, shot down by Erik.

When it was clear that the group had gone, Amelia turned towards Erik and whispered, "The day that James was shot. Are you sure he was, you know ... dead?"

Erik was taken aback by this unexpected question but then nodded. "I'm sorry Amy."

"It's just, well, he probably received the same treatment as me. You know – how my body can repair itself quickly."

"I know what you're thinking Amy," said Erik, grabbing hold of Amelia's hand. "And you're right. If you are shot then you can probably recover."

Amelia looked confused.

"I think you'd have to get the bullet out. But, more importantly than that," said Erik, "is that you need your brain and your blood system to remain intact."

Amelia started to say something but before she could form the words Erik interrupted.

"I'm no scientist Amy. But what I do know ... it's not magic, your healing. Whilst your heart is pumping your blood around your system, my understanding from what Sophie told me is that your cells – fibroblasts, I think they are called – work far more efficiently than in a healthy human. But once your heart stops pumping ... and, anyway, once your brain stops receiving oxygen you will suffer brain damage. It's permanent."

"With James? How did you know?"

"He was dead – I'm sure. I'm sorry but ... I'm sure he's gone Amy."

Amelia could not return to sleep and indicated that Erik should now take his rest. She offered to keep watch for the next couple of hours. Erik settled down into his sleeping bag whilst Amelia listened to the incessant scrabbling noise from the rats, which was growing in volume as the darkness deepened. The moon was bright now though, seeming to be suspended by invisible thread in an almost cloudless sky, and Amelia looked up at the stars and wondered which one, if any, of those in the sky was the planet Mars. In 2022, the year of the plague, a manned mission to Mars had been launched with the intention of forming a permanent settlement on the red planet. She wondered what had become of those brave men and women who, sleeping in their hibernation pods – identical to those that she and her family had used for twenty-five years – were hurtling away from the Earth at about three thousand miles per hour, as the virus ravaged life on the planet that they had left behind. Had they made it safely to the new settlement on Mars? If they had, they would have been confused when no communication from Earth followed them. They would probably think that there was a communication error because it would never had entered their minds that there was nobody left alive on the Earth to communicate with. Had Mission Control been able to send a message to them to explain something about what was happening on Earth? Amelia thought that was possible but maybe unlikely, such was the rapid deterioration in normal life as the plague swept across the planet. It also seemed improbable that any of the explorers had survived the last twenty-five years on Mars, especially given that they would have not received the scheduled shipments of equipment, supplies and reinforcements that they had been expecting. But just maybe they had survived. And just maybe they were looking up at the Earth from Mars now, wondering what had become of their home planet. Amelia liked to think that this was the case.

She shivered and then sensed someone behind her as Erik hugged her with both arms. She turned her head towards him and they kissed. Together they stood and watched the sky for a while in the dark. After a while, Erik suggested that since they were both awake and the moonlight was good they might as well continue on their journey towards Northumberland.

The scrabbling of the rats' nocturnal activities faded quickly away and a solitary owl's hoot hung on the cool breeze as they moved out under the silvery light of the moon and left the isolated outhouse behind.

CHAPTER 5

An overgrown footpath, that looked as though it had not been used in years, snaked between tall trees that rose from beds of green ferns. Amelia and Erik caught occasional glimpses of the sun, low in the sky, its early-morning light glistening off the damp woodland and catching sparkles in spiders' webs. It was a beautiful sight and Amelia's spirits were lifted. The forest was full of life and Amelia breathed in deeply as she walked, taking in the sweet, almost sickly, smell given off by the damp earth which combined with old fallen leaves and was rich in bacteria. As they walked, their feet crunched the moss and weeds beneath them, occasionally snapping twigs, making deafening cracks against the natural drone of birds chirping, occasional cuckoo calls and the incessant buzz of mosquito wings. It was difficult to move quietly and the denseness of the foliage limited visibility. The trees seemed to close in around them and the green canopy hung heavy above them. The woodland gave Amelia a strong sense of nature. It felt to her then as if the world was uninhabited, as if she and Erik were a modern-day Adam and Eve, exploring the world that was exposing itself to humans for the first time.

"Breakfast?" said Erik, gesturing to a large tree with huge gnarled roots above the ground that looked like they could be comfortable to sit amongst.

Amelia simply nodded and swung her backpack off her aching shoulder. She walked away from the tree to go to the toilet and, afterwards, searched for mushrooms. She had learned a great deal about mushrooms from Jill and Elizabeth, who she had met during her time in Conway. Mushrooms had not been a food that she had particularly enjoyed, in the old days. But these were harsher times and there were few foods now that she didn't enjoy. Besides, the way that Jill and Elizabeth had cooked them; they had given her a genuine liking for almost all types of mushrooms, especially fried. Her stomach made a gurgling noise and she had that unpleasant empty feeling, a feeling of nausea almost and she became more urgent in her search. Paying particular attention to the trunks close to the ground, she inspected several trees until, lodged within the crevices of a tree stump, she found an irregularly shaped yellow fungus that she recognised as chicken-of-the-woods. She tore a couple of generous handfuls of the mushroom away from their base. She knew they were safe to eat raw but with their fleshy, almost meaty texture would be even more delicious when cooked. She thought she heard a strange noise behind her – the breaking of a twig, perhaps. Something that didn't seem to fit into the eclectic, yet somehow harmonious, sounds of the woods.

Amelia showed Erik the spoils, asking whether they could risk a fire.

Erik looked around cautiously, staring for a while, high up into the canopy of the forest.

"Yes, I think we can," he said. "See if you can find me some large flat stones and some dry wood."

A few minutes later he laid the stones on the ground before building a loose pyramidal structure of twigs and small branches. Amelia was fascinated with what he was doing.

Seemingly satisfied with the structure, he pulled out a flint and steel set from within a pocket in his jacket and crouched down close to the ground. "We need to keep it as dry as possible," he said, in a low voice almost to himself. Then, in a louder voice, as if to explain to Amelia he said, "Wet ground and wet wood ... these generate the greatest amount of smoke."

He used the set to produce a spark close to the dry moss that he had placed at the base of the pyramid. "The canopy of the forest will give us quite a lot of protection though. It's a risk I think we can take." He lay low on the ground and blew the spark and it responded to his attention by flickering and crackling.

Once the fire was burning he placed the mushrooms in a small pan that he held over the flame. Within minutes the mushrooms turned black and started to give off a rich aromatic smell that made Amelia's stomach rumble. Eric added some water to the cooked mushrooms and stirred the mixture with a twig to make a sort of crude hot soup.

Once cooked, they left them to cool a little, whilst Erik kicked the fire over and then quickly smothered it with leaves and soil. The amount of smoke increased dramatically, but only for a few seconds, and then was gone. They ate the warm mushrooms directly from the pan with their hands, licking the juices from their fingers, before taking it in turns to sip the warm liquid that remained.

It felt good to have something warm in their stomachs and they rested for a while, enjoying the sights and sounds of the forest waking up. A bird flapped urgently somewhere high above them and branches rustled quickly. Erik looked up and thought he saw a squirrel disappearing behind a tree trunk as it clambered upward. From a distance they heard the distinctive cry of a cuckoo. They risked using a little water to wash and brush their teeth. Finally, they both sensed it was time to move again and they pulled their backpacks on.

"Put your hands in the air, slowly, if you want to live!" The voice was firm and hard and crashed above the soothing woodland sounds like the rattle of a snare drum. Neither Amelia nor Erik could immediately see who had spoken and they had no way to evaluate the threat. They both raised their arms slowly, instinctively turning to the left in the direction from which they had heard the voice, and saw three men walking slowly towards them. Each of the men had a bow with an arrow cocked, pulled back and ready to fire.

Erik recognised them from outside the barn last night. "Shit," he thought, quickly realising that they had probably been noticed at the barn after all.

"There are nine arrows pointing at you," said the middle of the three men, the same voice as before.

"He said don't move!" This was a different voice, this time from behind them. It was clear that they were surrounded and surrender seemed the only option available to them.

Amelia and Erik stood as still as they could as the men approached them cautiously. They could see five now but could hear several more behind them. The one who had spoken first was a substantial presence and evidently the leader. He was tall with a muscular build and had a large head, complete with a formidable forehead that slightly over-shadowed his cold blue eyes. Greasy light brown hair was pulled back into a ponytail, tied with a piece of black string. He stood just a few feet in front of them and stared directly into Erik's eye. "Check for weapons." His square jaw barely moved as he spoke.

The man next to the one with the ponytail moved towards Amelia and located her weapon, pulling it out of its holster. She thought about breaking his arm and smirked slightly at the idea but then thought better of it. Another man retrieved Erik's semi-automatic gun.

"Tie them!" The leader remained facing Erik as Amelia and Erik both felt their hands grabbed and pulled down behind their backs, before what felt like thin twine was wound tightly around their wrists. The rope pinched Amelia's skin and she gave out an involuntary shout.

"Ow! There's no need for that," she said.

The leader remained silent, still pointing his arrow directly at Erik's chest, until the two men tying the ropes were finished. Then he spoke. "Where are you from?" As he said this he pushed the point of his arrow onto Erik's chest.

Erik grimaced. "We're from North Wales. We're not looking for trouble."

One of the men laughed. He was short and stocky with untidy grey hair. When he laughed his lips parted to reveal yellow teeth that looked rotten in places.

The leader ignored his comrade and asked, "Why are you here?"

"We're heading for the government centre at Kielder Water," Amelia replied. "They have my father captive and we are going to get him back."

This brought a round of laughter from all of the men. Even the leader let a broad smile break out across his face, and he looked around at the men, enjoying the joke with them. At least some of the tension had been released.

The laughing subsided slightly. "And how exactly are you going to do that?" When the leader spoke his men were silent.

"We have already taken down the government centre at Anglesey," said Erik, maintaining eye contact with the man in front of him. "There were three thousand government citizens there but now the local people are in charge of the centre."

The man with the ponytail couldn't disguise the fact that he was impressed but he was also confused. He couldn't see how two people could achieve what they claimed. His uncertainty was addressed by Erik's next statement.

"We mobilised the local groups – we infiltrated their base – we lost a lot of lives ... friends and family. But we won."

"And you think you can do the same here?" the leader said, sneering slightly.

"Probably not." Erik showed no weakness as he maintained eye contact. "We're not sure what our strategy will be yet. We need to check out the surrounding land at the base."

"You don't want to go anywhere near Kielder Water," the leader said. He was studying the two captives intently, trying to weigh up how much of a threat they were. Meanwhile, Amelia tested her bonds and they gave slightly. She thought she could probably break free if she needed to. But the odds in a fight were not favourable, certainly not whilst Erik was still tied.

"My name is Erik and this is Amelia," said Erik. "Can we sit down and talk? We're no threat to you. There are things we know about the base at Kielder Water that might help you."

The leader was still calculating. He was the sort of man where you could almost see the wheels turning in his head, so transparent were his thought processes. After a few seconds he lowered his bow and relaxed his stance. He had decided that they were probably telling the truth.

"My name is Ethan. We'll talk. But back at camp."

"That's good enough for me," said Erik, smiling warmly before adding, "Any chance of taking off the ties? They're cutting off my circulation."

Ethan paused momentarily but then nodded. The stocky man with grey hair reluctantly untied the binds from the wrists of his two captives.

Ethan turned and set off. "Follow me." He walked briskly back in the direction from which he had come. Amelia and Erik followed close behind and after them came the other men including the ones who now had their guns. They walked for about three hours without break until, as light rain started to fall, they came to a small town seemingly in the middle of nowhere and dominated by grey stone buildings.

CHAPTER 6

Haltwhistle was an ancient town on the north banks of the river South Tyne, one of the two rivers that fed the Tyne that then flowed down to the North Sea at the estuary site of Newcastle-upon-Tyne. It was close to the site of the ancient wall, that used to be known as Hadrian's Wall, a defensive fortification in Roman Britain, begun in AD 122 during the rule of the emperor Hadrian. Part of the wall was still standing and Ethan led the group over it and down towards the town. Albeit now worse for wear, the wall had been there before modern civilisation and remained still, even as civilisation had come and gone.

The group followed Ethan to a church and through large wooden doors that creaked as they were pushed open. The cool air of the cavernous space soothed Amelia's face, warm from her exertions despite the light rain outside. She immediately noticed that the pews had been ripped out and in their place were ramshackle clusters of chairs and tables. It was clear that the area that had once been used for worship now fulfilled an administrative function for the group. Looking up, Amelia saw that huge stained glass windows were still intact at the end of the large space in which they now stood.

The group sat down together, glad to take the weight of their feet after their long trek, and waited until hot drinks were brought in on two trays. Amelia and Erik each took one. It was some sort of fruit or herbal tea, but welcome nonetheless after their walk.

Ethan took a mug of the steaming hot liquid and sipped it before saying, "We saw you in the old barn. We thought you were government agents." He seemed smug and was keen to tell Amelia and Erik how they had been tracked down. "So we followed you. We watched you have breakfast."

"We were so close we could smell it," said the man with the yellow teeth.

"And how do you know we are not government agents?" Amelia was feeling more confident now that both Erik and her were untied and that they no longer had several men pointing arrows at their faces. Erik cast her a glance as if to say, what are you doing?

But Ethan was nonplussed. "We don't," he said, "but we had heard about Anglesey and what you told us fits with the little we already knew."

Amelia turned towards Erik and gave him a little obviously fake smile before turning back to Ethan. "What do you know about Kielder Water? How many fighting units do they have?" Ethan blew his cheeks out and shook his head slightly. "We don't know how many," he said. "But you need to know that the situation here is quite different to the one you were used to in North Wales."

"How?" asked Amelia.

"As I understand it, in North Wales the government citizens mainly stayed in Anglesey and had little to do with the locals. Here they use the locals as cheap labour. Every man, woman and child over the age of twelve has to work for the government. In return each is granted enough food to live on, just. You haven't got a hope in hell of raising an army from them."

"What about you?" Amelia said between sips of the warm tea. "Are you part of that system?"

"Fuck No. We're too far away. Thank God. We sometimes manage to persuade people on the edges of their territory to leave and join us. Sometimes, people come here and seek sanctuary of their own accord. From time to time we come into contact with the government forces." He smiled. "It usually doesn't end well for them."

"So presumably sometimes ... locals enter the government base to engage in trade?" said Erik.

"Yep, that's correct. It happens all the time."

Amelia sensed that Ethan had already developed a certain amount of respect for Erik and was increasingly feeling confident that they were in no immediate danger.

"Well, that's our way in then," said Erik. "We simply walk in there as traders." He cast Amelia a sly wink.

"Yes, you can do that," said Ethan. "But it won't be easy. If you are caught they won't hesitate to kill you."

There was a silence and Amelia took a moment to take in the impressive interior of the church. There were two tall, but narrow, stained glass windows in front of her at one end of the church. Behind stone arches, which ran down each side towards where they sat, there were smaller stained glass windows, high up in the wall. It was obvious that though once a place of worship it was also very defendable.

It was Erik who broke the silence. "How many fighting men do you have here Ethan?"

Ethan sat with his hands on his knees, his knees spread far apart. He looked directly at Erik and said, "We can't tell you that."

Erik narrowed his eyes slightly and was about to say something when Ethan said, "But if you are still thinking about mobilising the locals as you did in North Wales you can forget it. We don't have anywhere near enough men. Nor do we have sufficient weapons even if we did have the men. Anyway, the entrance to the main base is always guarded by the machines. They are almost indestructible – arrows have no effect on them."

"Machines?" said Amelia. She had been trying to understand the story that the sequence of stained glass windows told, but now became interested in the conversation again.

"Androids," said Erik flatly.

"You know about these?" said Amelia.

"Yes."

"Explain!"

"Well, I've been to Kielder Water twice before remember. And we were shown the defence units then. Before the plague, Kielder Water was a military base and they were developing autonomous drones there for controlling urban areas where hostiles were suspected to be embedded, or where the locals themselves were hostile. The good news is that they only have about forty units."

Amelia's mouth nearly fell open. "Forty fucking killer robots. That you didn't mention."

"Yeah. I was going to mention it when we got closer."

Amelia was incredulous.

"You said you've been to Kielder Water?" asked Ethan.

"Yes," Erik replied and then paused before adding, "I was part of the government defence force at Anglesey."

Ethan visibly bristled at this information. "I thought you overthrew the government?" Ethan looked tense, as if he didn't know whether he could trust Erik anymore. Perhaps Erik was a government spy after all.

"It's a long story," said Erik.

"Well, let's hear it." Ethan was still not smiling. "We have plenty of time."

Amelia knew she had to be patient but she was worried in case time was the thing they were most short of.

CHAPTER 7

Sophie Wassall looked out of her office over clear blue water and wondered when Amelia would be coming. Not for the first time, she pondered this question as she sat in an office on the third floor of an impressive military building with a curved structure that followed the natural lines of the shore on Kielder Water, and which had four floors of offices and research laboratories. Kielder Water had been the largest artificial lake in the United Kingdom and was surrounded by the largest man-made woodland in Europe. It was a secluded location and ideal for the secret military establishment that had operated under the cover of a private electronics company. The research building sat between the water on one side and the barracks, now providing living accommodation for just over two thousand people, on the other side. Between the barracks and the research building was an inconspicuous two-storey building that was, in fact, the entrance to the underground block that had housed the residents during the purge. The block extended under the research building and some way out further under the lake itself.

The lake was also the site of the country's largest hydro-electric power generation plant and this now provided all the electricity required by the citizens of Kielder. Although not working at the levels it had done previously − when it had supplied the wider conurbation of Newcastle − the continual release of water into the North Tyne river still drove turbines that provided all of the electricity that Kielder water required. Electricity was also the power source for the autonomous machines, the so-called drone police that could operate for about twelve hours on a single charge.

Sophie squinted, her small brown eyes peering out through the glass as she thought she saw movement on the opposite side of the lake. It was gone now. It was probably just her imagination, she thought.

It had been a couple of months since her arrival here with Professor Savage and her assistant Jacob Scott. The president of Anglesey, David Talbot, had not survived the trip. The two helicopters had travelled together over the sea, passing west of the cities of Liverpool and Blackpool, but then, as they passed over the southern Lake District, the leading helicopter lost speed and altitude. Sophie saw the blades stall before slowly starting to rotate again. The helicopter became unstable, started to rotate quickly and plummeted to the ground, still spinning as it crashed into the side of a hill. Sophie had her helicopter circle briefly but when no survivors emerged from the wreckage she ordered her craft to continue on towards Northumberland. It was bad luck for Talbot, she thought. However, now that Anglesey had fallen she had no real use for him and as she sat back in her seat she thought it was probably for the best. Fate had at least dealt her a few good cards on this difficult day.

Anglesey had been lost but she still had Savage and she was on her way to arguably a stronger government base where a more aggressive position had been taken towards the scavengers. Talbot had always been too cautious whereas at Kielder Water they had taken a more proactive approach to working towards the new order. After all, there was a reason why some of the working classes had survived and that was to provide service.

Checking the clock on the far wall she noted that it was nearly three. She left her room and took the elevator up to the top floor where the office of Mark Bailey was situated.

Bailey was the president of Kielder Water. Before her arrival, Sophie had met Bailey on only three other occasions, twice whilst she had visited Kielder and once during his reciprocal visit to Anglesey. These had been exchange visits to swap intelligence and share knowledge. During those visits she had got on well with him and was confident that she would be received well on her arrival. She was correct. Bailey welcomed her to the team and realised that she had certain skills that it would be unwise to ignore. At Anglesey, Sophie had been in charge of security. Here she was initially given a special role to extract the vital knowledge that was believed to be in Savage's head. Savage had successfully treated his daughter Amelia and they needed him to explain to them where they were going wrong with their own, unsuccessful, attempts at gene treatments. She knocked on Bailey's door and waited until he called for her to enter.

Earlier that day she had been down to the laboratories to check on progress. On their arrival at the base, Savage had been transferred to a cell that was close to the research laboratories. One of her first orders had been to insist that Savage be tested; had he successfully treated himself? The tests had come back negative. This was a surprise and also a disappointment. Savage was also uncooperative in the extreme but this was a challenge to which Sophie was happy to rise.

Over the next four weeks she had tortured Savage on a daily basis. Inflicting pain upon him was her sole objective and something she thought about from the moment she woke up until when she went to bed. She often went to sleep thinking about new ways to hurt Savage. She took pleasure in using pliers on sensitive parts of his skin, holding hot metal probes to his body until his skin gave off an unmistakable stench of burning flesh, and whipping him until his skin broke in streaks of red and blue. However, the one consistent method she used was sleep deprivation. Savage's ankles were bound by a chain that was also attached to a metal ring in the stone floor of his cell. His arms were tied behind his back and attached via a rope to a mechanism in the ceiling. The contraption had been developed in late 2018 for interrogating prisoners brought here from the fighting in Israel. It had been rarely used over the next twenty-five years or so but was still in working order. A sensor was activated whenever the unlucky recipient of the treatment started to fall to the floor, which in turn resulted in the mechanism yanking the arms upwards causing pain, but more importantly causing the person to wake up instantly. For four days he had not been allowed to sleep. During the day he was regularly visited by Sophie and subjected to unspeakable punishment. At night he had respite from that at least, but no sleep. Actually, he did get some sleep. By the third day he started to experience so-called micro-sleeps where the brain shuts down for fractions of a second at a time, an involuntary process that prolongs life, but not an enjoyable one. It gave no relief from the sickening feeling of tiredness that Savage endured. During all of this time he was given plenty of fluids but minimal nourishment. On the fourth day he was finally untied and allowed to sleep. He fell into a deep sleep within seconds of being allowed to fall to the floor. Less than ten minutes later he was woken up as two guards poured buckets of cold water on him whilst another poked him with an electric cattle prod. Sophie got down on her haunches and grabbed his chin between her small fingers.

"Tell me, Savage. How do we apply the gene treatment you gave to Amelia?"

Over the next hour Savage mumbled about the science behind the treatment. He rambled and spoke incoherently at times, but there were also moments of surprising lucidity. The whole conversation was recorded so that it could be analysed later by the scientists at Kielder. Eventually, Sophie felt that she was only getting repeated information.

"Leave him there," she said. "We're through for now."

She walked over to the elevator and it opened to reveal her assistant Jacob Scott with another man, short and stocky and dressed shabbily. Sophie entered the elevator with them and tried to keep her distance from the short man, whose hair was matted and looked as though it had not been washed in weeks, as if he might be contaminated. However, as he spoke, his thin lips revealing yellow and broken teeth, a smile swept across Sophie's face. The elevator doors closed.

CHAPTER 8

The community at Haltwhistle consisted of about two hundred and fifty people. Despite being in the north it was in fact the exact geographic centre of the island of Great Britain; or at least, so it had been claimed. Before the purge, the population had been less than four thousand and only around fifty of those had survived the first onslaught of the virus. But it was a close-knit community and, certainly when compared with most of the cities, it had re-established some semblance of order very quickly. Here, the people supported each other and this in turn also drew in survivors from the surrounding countryside and even some who had fled, in panic and desperation, away from cities such as Newcastle-upon-Tyne. Survivors from Newcastle who quickly realised that there was nothing for them in the city had followed the river, staying close to the water. Some had settled in places such as Corbridge and Hexham. However, a few made it as far as Haltwhistle and over the years their numbers had accumulated.

The river South Tyne was an excellent source of fresh water and of food; there were huge salmon weighing over thirty-five pounds and an abundance of brown trout, sea trout and grayling. Ethan showed Erik and Amelia the small fishing industry that they had developed. The community also farmed sheep and a small number of cows, and grew crops quite extensively in the region. Fuel was limited however. Electricity was only available from wood- and peat-burning generators and these were used frugally to store food, provide lighting at night and during the winter months to provide heating to communal areas. Despite this, the group had a reasonable existence albeit living uncomfortably close to the shadow of the government centre further north.

Erik and Amelia were given lodging in a small cottage on the outskirts of the town. It was warm and dry, but there was no electricity and no running water. The residents of Haltwhistle each agreed to hand over everything that they produced, whether it be food, wool, alcohol or other craft products. They would meet each Friday morning in the church hall and food and other products would be distributed to them by the council. Each of the residents was known personally to the council and there was never any argument about how much each person would receive. The only valuable that was not considered to be owned communally was water. However, water was in abundant supply.

Erik and Amelia stayed two nights with the Haltwhistle community. On the third morning they packed and prepared for the fairly short journey that remained. Kielder Water was almost due north from Haltwhistle and the bottom of the lake was not much more than ten miles away. This now meant that they would reach the lake and follow its eastern shoreline before approaching the centre from the southeast whereas their original plan had taken them up the west coast of the lake before turning towards the east.

"Any chance of us having the guns back?" The guns had been confiscated and not returned and Erik had to raise this now.

"I'm afraid not." Ethan looked genuinely disappointed that he was going to hold the weapons back and added, "We need weapons to defend the people here and we don't get the opportunity to replenish our limited supplies often."

Erik accepted was he was saying and shook Ethan's hand. The two had developed quite a strong bond over the last two days.

Amelia gave Ethan a short but warm hug and they set off along the road. It was still a little grey but the rain had stopped. The road was framed by dry-stone walls on either side that threatened to be overrun by tall grasses and knotweed. They said little until the road came to an end and they had to start to cross the fields. It was Amelia who broke the silence.

"I was surprised you didn't insist on the guns. I'm assuming you have some master plan!"

"He wouldn't have given them to me no matter how hard I tried," explained Erik before adding, "Besides, he's right. They need the guns more than we do."

"You think so?"

45

"Certainly." Erik stepped over a wooden stile and landed on the other side before holding Amelia's hand to help her over, "A couple of guns aren't going to help us overthrow the city. Nor will they be much use against the robocops."

"Robocops?" said Amelia curiously.

"It was a 1980s sci-fi movie. If you missed it I guess you won't get the chance to see it now." Erik had seen the movie in the early years after the purge in the city of Anglesey. "The guns were only ever going to be of use if we came across rogue unfriendly locals. That doesn't seem very likely now."

"So how are we going to kill the robocops?" said Amelia, a little playfully.

"That's for me to know and you to find out." Erik smiled and took Amelia's hand. It was almost as if they were on a summer's day stroll without a care in the world. But ahead of them there was plenty to worry about.

"By the way, I never asked, how old are you Erik?"

"Thirty four," said Erik flatly.

"I was born forty-two years ago," Amelia said, smiling. "That makes me older than you."

"That's right," said Erik. "But only in terms of years."

"What do you mean?"

"You look eighteen and you behave as though you were eighteen." As soon as he had said it he realised he probably should not have done.

"What?"

"Sorry. But remember, you were asleep for twenty five of those years."

Amelia didn't say anything and just looked at the ground, inspecting the blades of grass, as they continued across the field. She let go of his hand. After a few moments Erik could stand the tension no longer.

"What's wrong?" he asked.

"Nothing." Amelia continued to look at the floor as they walked along.

"There is something wrong. Why have you gone so quiet?"

"I'm not quiet."

"You are," said Erik. He grabbed hold of her hand. "You're upset aren't you?"

"If you say so. You must know if you're such an adult."

Erik thought about this for a few seconds and then said, "It's what I said about you being young isn't it?"

Amelia didn't respond but bit her bottom lip as she continued to stare at the grass. Her cheeks reddened slightly and she began to feel slightly embarrassed about being so sensitive.

"I'm sorry," said Erik. He stopped walking and grabbed her other hand so that she was forced to stop walking too and they were facing each other. "Look," he said, "I didn't mean anything wrong. You look young. God, I wish I looked as young as you do. I can't help thinking of you as someone I'd like to protect."

Amelia opened her mouth to speak but Erik spoke first. "Yes, before you start, I know you are stronger than me. I know you don't need anyone to protect you. I love the fact that you are so strong. But sometimes, just let me have the fantasy that I am the man and the one who protects you."

Erik leant forward and kissed her on the lips and Amelia responded. They separated and Erik smiled. Amelia could not remain angry any longer and returned his smile.

"Race you to that gate!" Amelia said suddenly.

Erik grinned and said, "On the count of three. One! Two!" On the count of two Erik started sprinting towards the gate that was about eighty metres away.

Amelia was unperturbed and watched as Erik sped away. When he was nearly half way towards the fence Amelia set off. She easily reached the fence before Erik, with him about ten metres behind her. As he joined her she stretched out her hand to shake his.

"Bad luck!" she said.

"Congratulations," Erik said, shaking her hand. He was panting heavily and his skin glistened with sweat. By contrast Amelia was barely breathing faster than normal.

"I guess you're ... " Eric started to say but he didn't finish his sentence. Amelia rushed forward and put her hand over his mouth and hauled him to the ground. They landed close to the bottom of the hedge that was next to the gate.

Simultaneously Amelia took her hand off Erik's mouth and put a finger to her lips to indicate quiet.

Erik could hear the unmistakable sound of a helicopter. The sound grew louder and Amelia and Erik shuffled closer to the bottom of the hedge so that they would be difficult to spot. The sound intensified until it felt like it was right above them. Erik saw the craft pass almost directly overhead. It was no more than a hundred metres up and almost certainly undertaking some sort of reconnaissance. However, it didn't dwell in the area and continued on, roughly in the direction from which they had come. Gradually the sound died out.

Erik pulled himself up and Amelia joined him.

"That was close," he said. "Well spotted!"

"I don't suppose they were looking for us," said Amelia.

"No way," said Erik. "I don't see how they could possibly know we are in the area and approaching them. I guess it was just a standard reconnaissance trip. I am sure they keep a careful eye on everything within ten miles or so of their location. Remember, that's what we used to do."

As they climbed the gate and crossed two further fields, knee-deep in grass, Amelia recalled the reconnaissance trips that Erik used to undertake when they had first met. The sighting of the helicopter had brought to mind the seriousness of their situation and they continued in silence, both with their own private thoughts of what was to come. It was not until they reached a lightly wooded area that they relaxed slightly, in the knowledge that they now had cover from any further reconnaissance units, but visions of the future preoccupied them

48

still and weighed heavily on their mood. Light drizzle had started to fall and hung around them like a fine mist.

CHAPTER 9

"I can scarcely believe it," said Dr Meyer.

Sophie observed as the scientists watched the video footage that had been recorded of Savage.

"What do you make of it?" she asked, anxious for news that would indicate a breakthrough.

"I just can't believe it," repeated the man. He wore a white laboratory coat, a little stained and frayed at the cuffs, but which still managed to present a professional scientific image. His bony head had little hair, his face was pale and thin but his eyes, slate grey, constantly moving, betrayed his excitement.

"What does that mean?" said Sophie, impatiently. She wore a conventional two-piece blue suit – a tightly tailored jacket and a skirt that stopped just above her knees. Black two-inch heels completed her outfit.

"It's just I never imagined that it would be that simple. I don't see why we didn't think of that before."

"What?"

"The pH. It's the pH. By raising the pH of the donor solution it affects the three-dimensional configuration of the molecule so that ... "

"Spare me the details for Christ's sake. Just tell me. Will it work?" Sophie almost visibly tapped the point of her shoe on the floor as she became less and less tolerant of the scientist. She did not care two hoots about the pH. What she wanted to know was whether it would work or not. That was all that mattered to her.

"Yes, yes, it will work," said Dr Meyer. Dr Alex Meyer was the lead scientist for the genetics team. He had been personally working on the development of the treatment for twenty-five years and had almost given up hope that it could work in his lifetime. Now he could see that he had been missing something fundamental, but something so simple that it was extraordinary that he had not considered it before. Of course he cared about whether it would work. After all, he was in his sixty-third year.

The treatment would come just in time for him. However, at this time what he cared more about was the new knowledge, the scientific insight. He was excited at what he now understood. His mind was whirling at a million miles an hour and he could not wait to get into the laboratory to test the new ideas. Science was, after all, nothing if not empirical observation and testing of hypotheses. He never tired of telling people about his scientific hero, Albert Einstein, who had simply thought about the nature of light and in so doing had come up with his theories of relativity and special relativity with no empirical evidence. These theories had changed the world, slowly at first, but increasingly as the end of the 20th Century approached. Over the three decades following his seminal research papers he left it to others to carry out experiments, all of which confirmed that Einstein was correct. Einstein was special, without equal in Meyer's opinion. But Dr Meyer also understood that for almost all other scientists a hypothesis was just that – a hypothesis – until it could be backed up by observation. He therefore could hardly wait to test out his new hypothesis in the laboratory; however, in this case he just knew that he was going to have his hypothesis confirmed.

"It will? Are you sure?" Sophie just wanted to know the outcome. To say that she had little interest in the science was almost an understatement.

Dr Meyer looked at her and for a few seconds he seemed calm as he spoke. "Yes. I am completely sure this will work. We have the elixir of life."

That was almost a month ago. Now she was returning to the laboratory to check on progress in advance of her weekly meeting with Bailey. She asked Dr Meyer for an update.

"We've treated twenty-five scavengers and the therapy has been successful in every case," the doctor said.

"Any side effects?" said Sophie.

"No, none whatsoever."

She took the doctor to the side, away from his colleagues, and whispered something in his ear. He nodded and she smiled, as if pleased with the news.

She turned to leave the laboratory but suddenly stopped. Speaking directly to the doctor she said, "Dispose of all of the volunteers apart from two. Keep those for a longitudinal study of possible side effects."

Dr Meyer's face went pale at the thought of it and his mouth opened slightly but Sophie did not wait to hear what he was going to say and continued on out of the laboratory and towards the elevator.

"You heard her," he said to his colleagues. "Give lethal injections to twenty-three of the patients and move the other two to beds in the prison for long-term study."

"Which two should we keep?" enquired the laboratory superintendent.

Staring into the distance as if he had not heard the question Dr Meyer mumbled, "It doesn't matter."

"Enter!" It was the unmistakable tones of Mark Bailey. Sophie opened the door and walked through. She immediately saw the dark silhouette of Bailey, still sitting behind his desk, against the brightness from the window behind him. He was undeniably fat, with a double chin, though without being obese. Wiry white hair covered most of his head, apart from at the front where he had a high forehead, and crept down the sides in front of his ears as untidy sideburns. Perhaps his most notable features were his eyes, dark and deeply set, so far back that it almost looked like he had his eyes closed, below white bushy eyebrows. Despite his somewhat flabby appearance, he had a presence, an authority perhaps, that even Sophie respected.

As Sophie walked over he rose and they shook hands over his desk.

"How are you Sophie?" he said. When he spoke his voice was so low that it almost sounded as if something was moving, rattling, somewhere in his throat or perhaps deep in his chest.

52

"Fine. You?" Sophie smiled and tried to maximise her charm.

Mark simply gave the briefest of smiles and said, "Take a pew." He indicated the chair on the other side of his desk with his outstretched hand.

Sophie sat and crossed her legs.

She had a good view out of his window across the lake. It was slightly better than her view, with his office being on the top floor.

"Good news I hope!" said Mark.

"Very good news," replied Sophie, pleased to notice Mark looking at her thigh. "So far there have been twenty-five successful treatments. Success rate is one hundred per cent. No side effects."

"Impressive," said Mark. He paused as Sophie re-crossed her legs and then seemed to refocus as he said, "How long until we can offer the treatment to our citizens?"

"Well," said Sophie and then paused. She enjoyed making Mark wait for the next piece of information. Finally, she added, "I am having the treatment myself this afternoon. We can roll it out as soon as you are ready to make the announcement."

Mark was pleased but had a further question. "I remember you told me about the Savage girl. Didn't she have some enhanced ... features? Have we seen that in our patients?"

"No. We haven't." Sophie brushed the top of her thigh with her hand, bringing attention to it, and then turned her hand over, palm upwards, with her fingers bent inwards as if to inspect her nails. "None of our patients have shown any enhanced features as far as we can tell. You have to remember that after Sophie was treated she had twenty-five years in suspended animation. We don't know if there is a time delay before the genes fully express themselves or whether Amelia will be unique because of the unique circumstances in which she was treated."

Mark scratched the left side of his face with his hand and was having a conversation with himself inside his head, as if he was debating which of the options that Sophie has just outlined was the most likely. Then he said, "Well, since we will all live for the best part of a thousand years now we'll have plenty of time for that side of the treatment to be understood. We can wait."

"That is exactly what I was thinking," said Sophie, smiling broadly.

Mark stood up, moved in front of Sophie, and sat on the edge of his desk. "Well," he said, "I guess we can say that you have successfully completed the role we gave you when you came here."

Sophie continued smiling for a moment – just long enough, looking up at Mark – and then lowered her eyes in mock modesty.

"So we need to think of something else for you to do? Shall we have a conversation about that over lunch?"

"That would be a pleasure," said Sophie, accepting Mark's hand and standing up.

"Oh, by the way," said Mark, "What has happened to the girl's father, Professor Savage?"

"Him?" said Sophie almost as if she could not recall who he was. You don't need to worry about him. He's dead."

CHAPTER 10

Looking back, the woman estimated that at least four months had elapsed before she had an opportunity to escape. It was difficult to be sure – she had no writing materials to record the passage of the days. Each night she was locked in an attic room that contained a bed, a toilet pot, and very little else. Strips of wallpaper hung down, having peeled backwards from the top, and cast strange shadows when the moon shone through the skylight window. She had a pillow and a quilt on the bed; both were filthy. She doubted whether she could squeeze through the window and even if she did manage to it would be perilous to try to climb down the roof. During the first week she had managed to smuggle a sharp stone into her room and she used it to mark off the days by scratching small lines into the exposed plasterwork on the wall by the bed. According to these marks she had been held captive for 121 days. It was only an estimate though. There were days when she was so tired that she fell asleep before making a mark. She would sometimes wake up with the feeling that she had forgotten to make the mark the previous evening. But she could not be sure; and if she was not sure she did not make another mark. So the 121 days was an estimate, probably a lower estimate, she thought, using her scientific training.

The day that she had been captured was the worst day of her life. Since then, not an hour had passed that she did not mourn what she had lost, what she might be missing even still. In the mornings she was put to work by the river. She recognised it as the river Dee from her childhood and surmised that she was in Chester. In the mornings her work was to fish and to collect mussels and crabs, which she did to the best of her ability. Her ability was hampered slightly by the chain that was attached to her ankle at one end and to a metal ring on the harbour side at the other end. The chain was no more than twenty feet long. The ring was black iron and was one of those that used to be used for mooring boats in the days before the purge. She worked at the waterside from about six in the morning until about noon, by which time she was starving and grateful for the small meal of potato stew and bread that she was usually brought. There were days when her hunger got the better of her and she furtively slipped a fish into her pocket or even down her pants, which she would eat later, raw, when an opportunity arose. This only happened when she was desperate, however, since she knew that if she was caught the punishment would be brutal and without mercy. Her job was to collect fish and other seafood for the group, not to eat it.

During the afternoons she would be transferred to an allotment where she would gather crops, plant seedlings, and dig the land over. Again, she was shackled by the chain attached to her ankle, but this time it was attached to a vertical grey metal pole that was embedded in concrete. There were several such poles and the one she was attached to each day would depend upon which part of the land needed working. One of the poles was not quite as firmly attached to the ground as the others and sometimes, when she sensed that nobody was looking and she was close to the pole, she would lean on it with all of her weight and try to push it from side to side to weaken it at the base. It was hard going though. It was a couple of months or more – day 79 by her reckoning to be precise – before she sensed any additional movement at all.

In the evenings she was taken back to the living areas – a row of terraced houses that had been knocked through – where she was usually required to cook. Occasionally she was made to sleep with one of the men but this was fortunately a rare occurrence. The group understood that she was more valuable to them as a working slave and that if she became pregnant that would only lead to complications and could reduce production. When she cooked it would often be with three other women who were also held captive against their will. During cooking they had time to talk and she learned that they were put to similar work to her, though in different locations. She rarely saw them during the day. The three women were also considerably younger than she was and she sometimes wondered if this was why she was spared the unpleasantness of having to spend time with the men. Either way she was at least able to count her blessings on that score.

She was in her early fifties but she was not unattractive, with auburn hair and distinctive pale green eyes. During the day she carried out her duties as best as she could but inside her head she was in a very different place. She spent her time thinking about ways she could escape and when the scratches on the wall indicated that she had been a prisoner for 110 days she started to feel some hope; the grey pole in the allotment was showing signs of movement.

When she was free she headed west. It was not her preferred route but she knew she was on the north-west side of Chester and she did not want to head into the city. Her best chance was to escape to the countryside and hopefully find someone who was kind and would help her. So she headed into North Wales and along the coastal road. By the time she got to the outskirts of Colwyn Bay she was starving but still her instinct told her to avoid the town. She changed course and headed south. An hour later she collapsed, within sight of the river Conway. She had eaten little all day and she was also dehydrated.

It was fortunate that it was two girls who came across her body, collapsed on the banks of the river. One of them waited by her side while her sister went for help. Shortly later she regained consciousness in a cottage under the shadow of Conway Castle. Only after they had made her feel safe and relaxed, did the sisters ask her name. When she told them, their faces went pale with shock.

CHAPTER 11

It was when they were within sight of the lake that Amelia saw her first drone policemen.

Earlier as they made their way towards the forest, Erik had explained his plan. "Remember, when I didn't seem bothered about the guns we left with Ethan?

"Hmmm." Amelia was only half listening as she kicked stones along the dirt track that was leading them towards a copse of conifers.

"Well, that's because I knew we wouldn't be needing them." Erik copied Amelia and kicked a large roughly spherical stone that travelled some distance along the path before veering to the right and into the grass.

"And what makes you so sure?"

"Because we are going to approach the Kielder facility from under the water. We won't be needing guns there."

"What?" Amelia was suddenly listening to what Erik was saying with her full attention.

"You heard what Ethan said about the drones. Even if we had a couple of guns it isn't going to do us a lot of good. There are too many of them and they are too strong."

"But under water?"

"The lake is the one area they don't expect much of a threat from. We'll wait until dark and we can slip into the base. Hopefully, we we'll be in and out without being spotted. There are still a few securities to negotiate but I know how to get around those."

Amelia raised her left eyebrow. She trusted Erik. He had always been right but she was more than curious as to how this was going to work out.

It was mid-afternoon as they approached the lake area, careful to make as little noise as possible. Distant voices could be heard, drifting towards them in the breeze; instructions called out and banter between workers. They kept to woodland and away from roads and then found a position on the edge of the trees from which they could discretely observe. There were several fishing boats on the water and along the banks there were people with rods quietly fishing the shallow waters or handling crates which they would take from the water's edge and load onto the back of an electric cart that was parked on a track a short distance away.

The electric cart had a flat low compartment at the back and space for two drivers at the front. One of the drivers was still sitting in the cart and looked at first to Amelia to be wearing a white plastic suit. However, without warning the driver turned his head and stared directly in the direction of Amelia and Erik. Amelia was startled as she saw that there was a red band across where the eyes normally would be and that the face was unmistakably not that of a human. She felt Erik's reassuring hand on her shoulder and understood that they should stay still.

For what seemed ages the robot continued to look in their direction, the red light flickering across the horizontal visor. Amelia and Erik both tensed, preparing to flee, if necessary. The robot made a small movement as if it was about to step down from the driver's seat and at that very moment there was a crash that diverted its attention. Just behind the cart Amelia noticed that one of the crates had been dropped and had broken, spilling what looked at this distance like a containment of crabs. A second robot was now evident and was admonishing the worker who had dropped the crate. Two other workers ran over to assist, one bringing a new crate into which the three of them started shovelling the crustaceans. The driver robot was now out of the car and helping to supervise the clear-up operation.

Amelia now had the chance to observe the robots more closely. Her first observation was that they were tall; considerably taller than any of the humans around them. She estimated that they were probably at least two metres in height. They moved naturally almost as if they were humans inside lightweight spacesuits. They didn't seem to be carrying any weapons but Erik had previously told her that they had laser torpedoes built in to their forearms. Amelia had no idea what a laser torpedo was but it sounded formidable. At that moment Amelia had a sense of déjà vu and suddenly recalled her dream on the penultimate night in Anglesey. She realised that the drones looked almost exactly like those in her dream – or, at least, so it seemed. It was difficult to remember now exactly what they had looked like and she could not be sure that she was not having a false memory; but she had that feeling that she had seen them before.

She wondered how quickly they could move. It was hard to be sure, but she felt confident that she could outrun one in a straight race. However, she knew she would not be able to outrun the laser even with her meta-human speed.

They continued to watch until the spill was cleared up and the remaining crates were loaded. At that point the robots got into the seats at the front of the cart and drove it up a small incline and on to a road that meandered off to the east, following the shoreline of the lake. Erik pulled on Amelia's arm and they retreated back into the woods until they felt secure.

"Might as well get something to eat," said Erik. "We have quite a few hours to kill anyway."

Amelia pulled out a hunk of rough bread that was surprisingly pleasant, if a little dry, and started to chew on it.

"They look pretty formidable," she said. They were saving the few high-energy pouches that they had and instead were consuming the food that they had been given by the group at Haltwhistle. She drank copiously from her water container. Now that they were at the lake, lack of drinking water was not one of their pressing concerns. "The robots, that is."

"They are," replied Eric before taking a swig of water. He wiped his mouth with the index finger of his right hand. "Even if they didn't have any weapons I would struggle to match one in a fair fight. They're strong and they don't feel pain."

"But they're not indestructible?"

"Certainly not. There are several reports of them being incapacitated with well-aimed RPGs." He smiled ruefully. "You may have noticed we don't have any of those." Erik now took a bite out of his apple. His huge jaws broke the apple in two with no difficulty.

Amelia smiled and was reminded of how attractive he was when he was eating. She had finished her bread and was searching in her bag to see what else there was. There was a green crab apple. It did not look as ripe as it could have been but nonetheless she bit into it, albeit with difficulty. It was quite sour but she ate it all the same.

"I don't think any human has been able to defeat one of them in close combat though. You're like no other human of course, but I still wouldn't advise you to tackle one. If you see one coming towards you I would say run. Remember that even in close combat they can use their laser weapons."

They both finished their meal without speaking further. Amelia was wondering if she was stronger than one of the robots and was playing through various combat options in her mind. She knew that the task ahead of them was dangerous. It could easily be fatal. But it was worth it for the opportunity to rescue her father and visions of Sophie feeling the full fury of her wrath kept flickering through her consciousness as Erik lay back against a large tree stump and closed his eyes.

After a few hours Erik woke up and suggested that Amelia get some rest whilst he kept watch.

"What are we waiting for?" she asked him.

He was still a little sleepy. "We're waiting until it gets dark," he said quite slowly.

"Then what?"

"Then," he said, opening his eyes fully, "we're going to swim across the lake."

Amelia did not reply.

"You can swim can't you?" For a moment he wondered if he had made a major miscalculation – he had never considered the possibility that she could not swim.

"Yes, of course I can swim," replied Amelia. "How far is it across the lake? It looks an awful long way?"

Erik sat fully up. "The route we will take, it's about a kilometre. Is that ok?"

Amelia nodded and then lay flat on the ground and closed her eyes. It was going to be another hour or so before sunset and so there was nothing else to do. With any luck she would be seeing her father very soon.

CHAPTER 12

As the sun was setting behind them, Erik and Amelia made their way up the western shore of the lake. From here they could see the government facility almost directly opposite them. The curved front of the research facility reflected the last rays of the day's sun back towards them. Amelia had been a strong swimmer but it was over twenty-five years since she had last been in the water. Now she regretted not taking the opportunity to swim off the sea at Anglesey in the weeks following its downfall. Even in the summer months the sea off the coast of northern Britain could be chilly but she had seen many people taking advantage of the waters, despite the strong currents in the region, and enjoying themselves in and around the Menai Strait.

They waited until the last of the sun had gone and then slipped into the water, leaving their bags near some rocks where they might be able to find them later. It was far from certain they would be coming back this way though. The plan was simple enough. They would break into the facility and locate Amelia's father. Depending upon his health they would swim back over the lake and then head down south towards Haltwhistle, at least as a first destination; though it was clear that this was too close to Kielder Water for them to remain there for long. Haltwhistle was about as far as the robots could reach if they were to be sure of making it back to Kielder Water on a single charge so once they got beyond Haltwhistle they would start to feel safer.

That was the ideal scenario. Less ideal scenarios came into play if Professor Savage was too weak to swim across the lake. There were several possibilities then but perhaps the least hazardous would be to try to escape in one of the helicopters. Erik was an experienced pilot of course and he also knew where the helicopter pads were in relation to the research building. Any attempt to flee the facility by road would raise the possibility that they would run into the drone police and that was unlikely to end well for them.

Amelia trod gingerly as they walked out into the lake. The ground beneath was stony and slippery in parts and they were both careful where they put their feet. As the water level rose up to her waist Amelia shivered. It was cold, but not unbearable. They simultaneously stretched out with their arms and kicked their legs backwards. They both were wearing shorts, t-shirt and nothing else and they were able to swim easily; there was no tide and the water was calm. Fortunately there was little moonlight but there were nonetheless careful to make as little noise as possible. Amelia tried to slide through the water without making a splash. She quickly found herself some way ahead of Erik, her powerful arms able to pull her body through the water at a considerable speed.

Less than twenty minutes after entering the water, Amelia was able to put her feet down and touch the bottom on the other side. The ground was soft and sandy and gave slightly beneath her. She stayed in the water, with just her head on top, waiting for Erik to catch up. He was about five minutes behind but soon they were standing together up to their necks in the cool dark water. Erik was blowing hard but as usual Amelia seemed barely perturbed by the exercise.

Ahead of them was a sandy beach at the top of which was the research facility. To the right, as they looked, there were some trees and Erik had already indicated that they should make for those. Erik motioned that they should stay in the water and move to the right so that they were closer to the trees.

"There are motion sensors that cover the beach in front of the research labs. We need to approach the trees from over there." Erik pointed to a point that was about thirty metres south.

Amelia nodded and followed Erik through the shallow water.

When they had reached the target point they moved quickly out of the water and towards the trees.

"We need to wring out our clothes," said Erik. As he said this he took off his t-shirt and then stepped out of his dripping

64

shorts. Amelia followed likewise and they wrung and squeezed the garments to get them as dry as they could. Erik gathered together the clothes and spun them around his head; water sprayed in all directions and Amelia had to put her head down to keep the water from her eyes.

"That's the best we can do," said Erik. He passed Amelia's clothes to her.

Amelia pulled the shorts on. They were still damp but at least not dripping too much water. It was quite uncomfortable pulling on the cold, wet t-shirt and as it clung to her body it was unpleasant where it touched her skin.

Erik dressed and then sat down on the ground. "Let's give it an hour or so. We have no rush and it makes sense to let our clothes dry as much as possible."

Amelia said nothing but sat down next to Erik and snuggled under his arm. She was shivering and wanted to be closer to his warm body. She let her head rest upon his shoulder and chest and half closed her eyes.

"Erik?"

"Hmmmm."

"Tell me about your sister," said Amelia, and then before he had chance to protest, "I really want to know."

"She was called Ceri. She didn't make it to the bunker."

Amelia sat up with a jolt. "What?"

"She didn't make it. Or, to be more precise, we didn't wait for her."

Amelia squeezed his arm with her hand, encouraging him to go on.

"On the day that we were meant to go to the bunker, it was raining and cold. It was in the early days of the plague. Things were not too bad. You know, when people still had no idea how serious things were going to become. Our parents had told us not to go out, that we were going away on a long trip, and that a car was coming to collect us after lunch."

"You didn't know you were going to the bunker?"

"Not then. We were too young to really understand what was going on. But we knew that we were going to go away for a long time and that we might not even be coming back. I think Ceri sensed that more than me, anyway, looking back on things." Erik paused, as if thinking back all those years ago was an effort. "Ceri had a friend, a girl called Alwen. They were best friends. You know how girls are that age."

"You were what, ten? Was she younger?"

"No, we were twins. Like you and James. How strange is that?"

Amelia was too shocked to speak. She had never imagined this.

"I think she wanted to see Alwen one more time before we went. She ignored what dad had said about staying in and about the car coming promptly at 2pm. When we noticed she was missing my mum went mad. Totally ballistic. She went round to Alwen's house, it was on the next street. Ceri had been there but she and Alwen had gone out. They couldn't have gone far. Nobody was going out much in those days for fear of catching the virus. They probably were in the park or maybe in another friend's house nearby." Erik's voiced trembled and as he continued Amelia could see he had tears forming, "The thing I could never forgive," he said, "was that my parents didn't wait for her. When the car came and she was not there there my dad ... he insisted that we go. I remember I cried all the way as the car drove along the coast road to Anglesey."

"I can't believe it," said Amelia. "A parent would never do that."

"You didn't know my father," said Erik, without emotion.

"Well, I suppose my own father faked his own death and led us to think he was dead. So I guess I shouldn't be surprised."

"You can't compare the two men. My father was a bastard. Only interested in himself and power."

"But what about your mum?"

"She was upset, naturally. I blame her just as much because she went along with it. She didn't stand up to him. But at least she insisted that later that day they sent a car back, and when that came back empty, they sent another back the next day."

"They didn't find her?"

"They found her. But by the time she got to Anglesey she had the rash. Everyone coming to Anglesey had to go into three days' incubation before being allowed into the block. She never came out of that."

"You don't know what happened to her?"

"Not for sure. I never saw her body. I guess ... I was ten – too young."

"So do you think she would have had the plague even had your parents found her that day?"

"I don't know. We'll never know. All I know is that my father cared more about his career than about his family."

Amelia squeezed Erik's arm again and said, "I'm so sorry, Erik." She snuggled into him to keep warm and closed her eyes.

Nearly an hour later Amelia woke up to the feeling of cold and clammy clothes but Erik suggested that they were dry enough to begin the next phase of their expedition.

"You ok?" she asked.

Erik just nodded. He was in a different mode now that they were beginning their mission. He was reasonably familiar with the security features of the base from when he had visited there before. He knew the beach was covered by motion detectors but there was an underground passageway that exited the ground close to where they were now.

Using his feet to sweep leaves and loose branches out of the way, Erik was walking around in the vicinity looking at the ground. Finally, he knelt down and used his hands to brush away some loose sand.

Amelia saw that there was a man-hole cover in the ground. It was circular and slightly concave with a cross-bar that cut across its diameter. Erik squatted next to the hole and grabbed the bar with both hands. He started to twist but the bar did not move. The exertion made him grunt and his face reddened but still there was no movement. He let the bar go and exhaled.

"It's tight," he said. "I guess it's not been opened for a long time."

Amelia squatted down on the opposite side to him. "Allow me."

She grabbed the bar with both hands and twisted. For a second there was nothing and then it gave slightly and there was a faint grinding noise.

"Slowly," said Erik, "and quietly."

Slowly, Amelia turned the bar until it had completed a ninety-degree turn and then it stopped.

"Try lifting it," said Erik.

Amelia pulled upwards and straightened her legs, easily lifting the cover from its casing. It was made of metal and about six inches deep. Erik inspected the edges.

"Rust. No wonder I couldn't turn it. It had rusted over. Obviously hasn't been opened in years."

"You're just weak," teased Amelia, smiling.

Beneath them was a small hole but peering down it was black. Erik unzipped a pocket in his shorts and pulled out a tiny torch and used it to illuminate the hole. It was a tube, a similar size to the cover, and down one side there were indentations that would serve as a ladder. The floor looked to be about twenty feet down.

Erik went first, lowering himself into the cylindrical hole and descending via the rungs. Amelia had a flashback to the entrance to the bunker in her house. The entrance facing her was of an almost identical construction.

"Follow me." Erik's voice was quiet but had an echo quality about it. "And try to put the cover back on."

Amelia lowered herself into the hole and, when she was down about as far as her upper chest, she pushed her bottom against the far wall to keep from falling and pulled the cover back over the entrance. It was pitch black but then Erik turned his torch back on and was shining it upwards to illuminate the rungs for Amelia.

At the bottom, a ladder extended from the hole in the ceiling to the floor. They found themselves standing in a tunnel. They were at one end and there was only one direction to go. Erik swept the light from his torch from side to side so that they could see more. There was a small amount of brackish water at the bottom but apart from that the tunnel was unremarkable.

Erik lead the way and it was not long before they came to a door that blocked their way forward. In the centre of the door was a wheel and it was obvious that turning the wheel would open the door. Erik cupped his hand to the door and tried to listen. The last thing they wanted to do was fall through into an occupied room. There was no sound, but then Erik was not sure how thick the door was.

This time he stood aside and gestured for Amelia to open the door.

Gripping the wheel she turned it anticlockwise. It moved effortlessly and as she pushed, the door opened up into a dark room. Erik used his torch to illuminate ahead but it was only possible to see the floor for a few metres.

They stepped inside. They had only walked a few paces when the lights came on and they were so bright that for a second or two they were almost blinded; like the experience of coming out of a dark cinema into the light of a bright summer's day. Amelia was the first to open her eyes and what she saw made her feel sick in her stomach. They were not alone.

CHAPTER 13

The two girls placed the woman in an armchair and sat with her until she regained consciousness. They gave her a glass of water and reassured her when they saw panic on her face as she realised that she was in a house. For a second she thought she had been recaptured.

"You're ok – just relax. You're safe here," said Elizabeth.

The woman sipped on the water and stared furtively around her. Her lips were dry and cracked and her hands shook as she held the glass. She didn't recognise where she was but the two young women seemed friendly enough. Her heart rate started to slow as she realised she was safe.

Jill held the woman's hand and introduced themselves to her, before asking the woman's name.

"Lilly. Lilly Savage," the woman said, croaking on the last word, before taking another sip of water.

"Lilly Savage?" said Elizabeth. She looked at her sister, Jill, who seemed to be equally taken aback by the revelation. It was a huge surprise to hear that name. But now that they had heard it, the physical resemblance to Amelia was striking.

"Yes. I am looking for my family. Have you heard of them?"

"Your daughter," said Elizabeth, "what's she called?"

"Amelia. My son is James."

"We know Amelia. She was here not long ago." Jill could not contain her excitement and had to tell Lilly what they knew. She was also excited for Amelia who she knew would be ecstatic when she learned that her mother was alive and well.

"She was here? When?"

"Well, a month or so ago. But we saw her a week ago in Anglesey. She's probably still there."

Lilly sobbed with happiness. "Are you sure?"

Elizabeth put her arm around Lilly and gave her a reassuring squeeze. "Absolutely sure. It's definitely her. Apart from anything else, she looks just like you."

Elizabeth smiled between the tears.

"She was in an underground pod thing, in Manchester, for twenty-five years. That's her isn't it? Not many people have a story like that." Jill said, beaming, as she got up and left the room.

"I can hardly believe it. I need to get there as soon as possible." Before the plague, of course, there were mobile phones. Now there was no way to contact Anglesey, no way to get a message there other than to travel there. There was not even a conventional telephone network.

"I know," said Elizabeth. "We'll take you there. We have transport."

"Thanks. Can we go today?"

"You need a good meal first and a rest," said Elizabeth. "We can go tomorrow morning, first thing. Ok?"

Lilly nodded and wiped the tears from her eyes using the sleeve of her cardigan. "Is she ok?"

Elizabeth bit her lip and then said, "She's ok. There's just one thing ... It's possible she may already have left Anglesey – your husband, Jon, has been taken captive and Amelia was planning on a rescue mission."

"What? That can't be right – Jon died. I saw his body."

"Well, it turns out that wasn't his body," said Elizabeth.

Lilly was bewildered. It was fantastic news that Jon was still alive, if it was true. It was hard to believe though. How could it be possible? But she immediately worried about him. "You said he was captured. Who by? Where is he?" She had so many questions.

"That is a very long story," said Jill, who had returned with a mug of soup which she handed to Lilly, taking the empty water glass in exchange, saying, "It's not very hot, I'm afraid, but it'll do you good. We'll tell you everything you need to know whilst you get cleaned up and have a good meal."

Lilly greedily drank the warm soup. She drained the mug and then sank back in the armchair. She suddenly realised how tired she was. Her eyes were so heavy.

Elizabeth took the mug from Lilly's hand and placed it on the small table by the side of the armchair.

"There's one more thing you need to know about your daughter. She ..." started Elizabeth, before realising that Lilly was fast asleep.

CHAPTER 14

Amelia and Erik were both disorientated and shocked, to the extent that it took them a few moments to take in what they were seeing. They were in a room with white walls and ceiling. It was so bright it was hard to see things clearly. When their eyes had adjusted, they saw Sophie standing opposite to them and next to her was a man, looking out of place because he was scruffily attired whereas Sophie was dressed immaculately as usual. Either side of them were two of the robot police. Halfway between Sophie and Amelia were two more robots, one on each side of the room. Amelia turned to look at Erik and noticed that there was a robot in the corner by the wall through which they had emerged. She did not need to check to know that there was also one in the opposite corner, near to her. Six drone police, armed and highly dangerous.

"Welcome to Kielder Water, Amelia," said Sophie.

Nobody had ever defeated one of the drones in single combat, never mind six of them at once. For a second she thought of turning around and running back through the tunnel. She thought she might be able to make it. But Erik must have sensed her intentions because he put his hand on her forearm as if to say, don't move. His instinct was right. As she thought about it more it was clear that they were helpless. Six weapons were directed at them and the robots could fire in a fraction of a second.

"Close the door Liam," commanded Sophie.

The short man shuffled across the room and towards where Amelia and Erik were standing. As he passed them he gave Amelia a sly wink and in that moment she recognised him.

"You!" Amelia could not contain her surprise.

"You know him?" said Erik.

"You don't recognise him? It's one of Ethan's men. One of those that caught us in the woods."

"That's right darling," said Sophie, looking pleased with herself. "It's surprising what people will do ... for a little bit of extra food. Liam handed you two over for a sack of potatoes."

Liam went behind them and closed the heavy door, turning the wheel mechanism to lock it with a little difficulty.

"Now, Liam, tie their hands."

Liam grabbed Amelia's wrists and pulled them behind her back. He fumbled in his pocket and brought out some thin rope that he wrapped tightly around her wrists. The cruel binds immediately cut into Amelia's flesh and she winced.

"Not too tight this time, I hope," said Liam.

Amelia ignored him and Liam repeated the operation with Erik.

"Follow me," said Sophie.

Liam nudged them both forward and they walked towards Sophie who turned and opened a door at the far side of the room. They walked down a short corridor to an elevator. The elevator took all four humans and two of the androids; the other four androids remained below. The elevator rose and opened to an office environment. Sophie led the way down the corridor and opened a door that led into her office.

She went to her desk. As she did so she turned and said, "Liam, you can go now. Come back when you have something else valuable to tell me. Until then, stay away."

Leaning back in the chair behind her desk she indicated that Amelia and Erik should stand in front of the desk. The androids stood near to the door, making any possible escape unthinkable.

Amelia glanced out of the window and, although it was dark, she could make out a grass lawn below, illuminated somewhat by the office lighting from the building. It looked as if they were a couple of floors up, maybe three.

Sophie shuffled in the chair to get comfortable.

"I knew you would come," she said. "I knew you would want ... retribution." She paused, briefly, before overly enunciating the last word.

74

Amelia strained her hands behind her back and felt the rope give a little. "I just want my father back. Let him go and Erik and I will walk out of here."

Sophie laughed. "It's too late for that Amelia."

"It's not too late. Let me speak with him. I can persuade him to tell you what you need to know."

Sophie paused for a fraction of a second before delivering her reply. "I already know what I need to know. Thanks to what he told us we have perfected the treatment."

The information sank in and Amelia was speechless.

"That's right." Sophie pushed her chair back a little and crossed her legs. "We have already treated over fifty citizens. I was the first."

"You?"

"That's right. You're not the only immortal Amelia. Not anymore."

Amelia pulled her wrists apart and twisted her arms. The ropes were definitely loosening and she was sure that she could break them. She looked over her shoulder and saw the two androids. They were motionless and there was no indication that they were active, apart from a flickering of the red band across their eyes. But Amelia was sure that they would react the second she was free.

"I'm going to live for a thousand years," said Sophie. "Longer, of course, because by then we will certainly have reached the technological singularity even given the hiatus we have suffered because of the purge."

"The technological what?" said Erik.

The point where computer advances and bioengineering will be such that anything will be possible. By then we'll be able to make new bodies, new organs, new brains. We may even download our consciousness into androids like that." She gestured over to one of the androids but it made no response, nor even any indication that it had heard.

"You really believe that," said Erik.

75

"Certainly I do. Did you know that in the years leading up to the purge, scientists predicted that we would have reached it by 2045. That was in less than a quarter of a century's time. It's understandable that progress has been put back, of course. But by 2100? By 2200? Certainly. And I can wait."

"You're crazy," said Amelia.

"Maybe. And you, Amelia, are lovely. I would have liked to have been your friend. You could have had a great future. A really great one. But, now, I can't let you live. You know that, don't you?"

"I don't really care about that. Take me to my father. You don't need him anymore."

"You're right. I don't need him. But I am afraid that he didn't give the information we needed willingly. He needed to be persuaded."

"You better not have hurt him. Take me to him now!" Amelia could feel her anger rising. Her face reddened and she strained again at the rope restraining her wrists. "If you have hurt him ..."

"Quite," said Sophie, "and that is exactly why I cannot let you live. You will always want your retribution." Sophie smirked, letting this sink in. "He's dead Amelia. Your father is dead."

"Nooooo." Amelia started to cry but she was also angry. "I don't believe you."

"Your father was a very important man Amelia. He will always be remembered. He created the elixir of life."

Sophie opened one of the buttons on her blouse and pulled out something on a chain. "That is why ... I wanted to be the one to keep a part of him. What stories I will tell about this thousands of years from now." She revealed a small white structure on the end of the chain that hung around her neck.

"What is it?" asked Amelia, between sobs.

"It's a little memento."

Amelia looked more closely. It was a circle and inside the circle was the letter h followed by a plus sign."

Sophie proudly displayed it, leaning forward over the desk so that Amelia and Erik could better see it.

"It's exquisite isn't it? Handmade. It's the symbol for transhumanism. I had it made from a piece of your father's skull; he will be forever remembered as the father of transhumanism."

Amelia screamed and as she did so she brought her arms forward, the ropes holding them snapping as effortlessly as if they were tinsel wrapped around a Christmas tree.

Sophie jumped back into her seat. The two androids made a half-step forward.

"No, Amelia. No." It was Erik's voice.

Though Amelia's eyes were flooded with tears, her lower eyelids falling under the weight of the water and her head screaming inside with anger, something about Erik's voice caught her attention and she looked at him.

For a few seconds she looked into Erik's eyes. In an instant she recalled that her brother, mother and father were all dead. She also saw that Erik loved her as much as anyone ever had. And she understood that if anyone were to seek retribution then it would have to be her. This was not the time to throw her life away. She also saw that Erik had a plan and he flicked his eyes leftwards momentarily. She thought she understood.

Erik turned and stepped towards the androids.

"Look," he said. "There is no reason for anyone to get hurt." He got up close to one of the robots and almost pushed his face into that of the android.

The android reacted by placing both hands on Erik's chest and pushing him backwards. Erik was flung backwards and crashed into the desk.

But whilst this was happening the androids were not watching Amelia and she somehow had known that Erik was going to make this distraction; that he was going to sacrifice himself again so that she could live.

As Erik was pushing towards the android, Sophie saw Amelia move. She moved more quickly than Sophie had ever

77

seen any human move before. She sprinted the few yards to the window and threw herself at it. Her outstretched fists hit the glass first and it shattered.

Amelia had realised that had she tried to kill Sophie she probably would not have succeeded before being killed herself by one of the androids. Dealing with Sophie would have to wait for another day. For now, the best thing she could do was to escape and the window was her only option. She had not known whether she would be able to break the glass. For all she knew it may have been security glass. But the window shattered into a million pieces and she literally flew through it into the cold black night.

It seemed as though she hung in the air for ages. Maybe it was her imagination but she almost had time to feel the coolness of the evening air on her skin. It also seemed as if the grass was dark grey rather than green and this puzzled her. Perhaps it was to do with the lights. She remembered reading somewhere, decades ago, that the colour of things depended upon the light they were viewed in. After a while she understood she needed to think about how to land. The idea that she could land on her arms and do a forward roll was in her mind.

She hit the ground quickly with a thump. She heard a cracking noise and realised that she had probably broken her left arm. She wondered why she could not feel any pain. But she did manage a forward roll, of sorts, and immediately jumped to her feet. She sprinted to the lakeside and into the water but did not stop; her legs continued to pump until the water was almost to her chest, at which time she threw herself forward. Ignoring the searing pain that was now in her forearm, she swam out into the lake. By the time the androids had got out of the building and were on the lakeside, Sophie behind them screaming out instructions, she was already at least a third of the way across the water.

The androids fired into the water and Amelia was aware of lights and hissing sounds as the lasers penetrated the water around

78

her. Then she felt a burning sensation on her right calf and realised that she had been hit.

CHAPTER 15

The drones were unable to enter the water and Amelia was putting yards between them and her with each and every stroke. Sophie seethed with anger as she saw Amelia's body diminishing in size, rapidly approaching the far shore. She instructed the drones to the roof and to the helicopter pads.

Meanwhile, Amelia made it to the far shore and dragged herself out of the water, running without pause to take cover amongst the trees. Her arm was heavily bruised and almost certainly broken but at least it did not seem to be a compound fracture. It would heal, in time, and although the pain was now almost unbearable it was the least of her concerns. If she had to fight one or more of the drones now her chances would be even smaller than they would have been if she had not been incapacitated. The pain in her left leg reminded her she had been hit and she grimaced as she saw the patch of raw flesh.

Panic momentarily flashed across Amelia's face as she heard the unmistakable sounds of helicopters. She looked across the water and saw at least three bright lights heading towards her. Moving quickly she drove deeper into the forest. Even as she did so she was thinking about the possibility that the helicopters were equipped with infrared night-vision cameras; if they were she was in deep trouble.

Ten minutes later she could still hear the helicopters but they were not getting closer. She guessed that they were scanning the periphery of the woodland, hoping to catch a glimpse of her as she exited into more open areas. After a short while, she stopped and collapsed on to the ground. There was no immediate threat and she wanted to inspect her wounds more carefully. Her arm was discoloured but there was no sign of the skin being broken which was a good sign. She tried to move her fingers and she was able to do so, although she winced in pain as she did it, but clenching her fist was too painful to even attempt. Turning to her leg, she noticed that the skin on her lower leg, below the knee, seemed horribly burnt. However, the damage was mainly superficial. She was confident that both injuries would heal but it would take a day or two, maybe more. Meanwhile, if she had to fight the drones she would be doing so effectively with one hand tied behind her back. It was not a confrontation that she was looking forward to. Hiding and running; these seemed to be her best options at the present.

Voices, distant but unmistakable, made her glance behind her and she saw several beams of light moving in sweeping arcs between the trees. They were following her into the forest. With this realisation she got back to her feet and started to jog away from the lights. As she picked up speed she still heard occasional voices but they seemed to be getting further away. She had been running along a rough track but she decided that this might not be the best option and veered off to the left, pushing through undergrowth, ignoring the pain she was feeling from her bare feet as she trod on rough branches and pine cones.

After a while the forest started to thin and the undergrowth became lower until she was walking on grass between occasional pine trees. Ahead were several open fields that she would need to cross before she could plunge into what looked like a small but dense copse. For a while, she hesitated. Leaving the cover of the trees was a risk but it was one that she was probably going to have to take sooner or later. Certainly she had to take this risk whilst it was still dark. It was unfortunate that the sky was still relatively cloudless and the moonlight was quite bright but it was preferable to being exposed in full daylight. She didn't know how many men Sophie had at her disposal and how likely it was that she could encircle the forest and trap her. It was not a possibility that she was prepared to face and she took a deep breath before sprinting out into the open space.

She had been running for about twenty paces when she saw a bright light and heard the sound of the laser cutting into the grass around her. She looked around and saw two drones closing in from the right. It seems they had been stationed on the edge of the forest and had been waiting for her to make a move. Using all of her super-human ability she accelerated down the hill and headed for a gap in the stone wall that separated one field from the next. Breathing heavily she reached the gap and could see the treeline at the bottom of the next field. But as she ran though the gap she slipped on the mud and lost her footing. Out of control, she careered into the wall, barely having time to put her arms out. Hitting the wall with a sickening crunch, she cried out in pain before coming to rest on her stomach in the mud. There was no part of her body that was not in pain but she did not have time to even evaluate her injuries. She knew she must get up, quickly, but she was groggy and disoriented. She managed to turn over and saw the drones closing in. They were less than twenty feet away. As she thought about her fate she felt surprisingly calm. This was it. She had had a good run but there was no way out of this situation. Somehow the recollection of a dream she had had about a young girl being chased by robots flashed through her mind. Was it a premonition? Or just a coincidence?

Her only hope was that the drones had been ordered to capture her rather than kill her, but she realised that this was unlikely. Sophie had made it clear that she intended to kill her and there was, after all, no reason to keep her alive now that they had already mastered the gene treatment. She could try to fight the drones but she was badly injured, she had no weapons, and her adversaries were heavily armed and stronger than any man. Everyone dies sometime, sooner or later. This was her time. She saw one of the drones move its arm as if aiming the laser weapon towards her and as it did so she closed her eyes.

She heard a loud sizzling sound but several seconds later realised that she was still alive. She was not experiencing the intense, but hopefully brief, pain that she had been anticipating. In fact, she had not felt anything at all. She opened her eyes and saw both drones lying on the ground, motionless. What the fuck, she thought. How had that happened? A voice behind her shattered her thought processes and she quickly turned around to see a small group of half a dozen people or so standing just on the other side of the stonewall. One of them was holding a huge weapon. It was so large that it had wide straps that went around the shoulders of the woman who was carrying it. It was obvious that, whatever this weapon was, it was responsible for taking out both of the drones with a single shot. Amelia stared in disbelief. A minute ago she had believed she was going to die and then, almost out of nowhere, this woman had appeared and had turned things upside down. But that was not the reason she was shocked. In fact, she was not even thinking about the drones or her near-death at all. Tears filled her eyes and all she could manage was a single word.

"Mum?"

CHAPTER 16

The chain jerked upwards and the pain in Erik's arms and shoulders jolted him awake just as he was losing consciousness. He had no idea how long he had been hanging there. Certainly for days. The day after Amelia's escape he had been visited in the cells by Sophie who had insisted he tell her where Amelia was headed. The truth was he did not know. The only place he could have given her was Haltwhistle; but then, she already knew about that thanks to her spy Liam. But he resolved not even to give this piece of useless information. Sophie made a half-hearted attempt to force the information out of him. Using a pair of pliers she cut the little finger off his left hand. He screamed in agony but refused to speak otherwise. It did not surprise Sophie and she resolved to soften him up using the rack. Now, as he hung there, the pain in his hand was long forgotten as he longed for sleep to overtake him.

In a state of half sleep he dreamed about Ceri and the day that she arrived at Anglesey. She stepped out of the back of the car and walked over to the men in white suits who were waiting to greet her. The face region of the suits were constructed from a clear plastic visor which was slightly misted so that it was hard to see the features of the men behind them. As one of them put his hand on her shoulder to guide her into the door of the incubation room, her cardigan fell from her and revealed her arms. The man stepped back as he saw a rash of red and brown marks on her arm. There was shouting and people moved quickly. Suddenly, she was being shunted in a different direction, towards a black van with no windows. One of the men opened the back doors to reveal two benches running down either side of the van. Seated on the benches was a group of sorry individuals who seemed resigned to their fate. On the right, a mother held her young son, who was crying, and tried to comfort him. On the left, a young couple held hands, looking into each other's eyes, trying to find some pleasure at least in these last moments, before the virus in their bodies made life intolerable and then, after a few days, death welcome. Ceri screamed as she realised what was happening. She was going to be put into that van and taken away from her family. She struggled with the two men who now held her and tried to tell them that she was healthy. The marks on her arm were not the rash; they were a henna tattoo. She and her friend had just got the tattoos – matching ones – as a way to remember each other. She tried to rub the tattoo off but the men were not listening. As they effortlessly lifted her young body into the back of the van an old man, towards the front of the van, only half visible in the dark, vomited all over the floor. Ceri screamed again and pulled at the mask of the man who was pushing her further into the van. The condensation cleared and she saw her father's face, cold and emotionless, seeming barely to recognise her.

The chain jerked and Erik regained consciousness.

Erik screamed as searing pain shot down his arms and rippled across his upper back. Sweat covered his face and dripped onto the floor in front of him. He was naked and his arms were pulled back behind him in a painful configuration; however, this was nothing when compared to the pain that was induced when the system sensed that he was falling to the floor, as he fell asleep. His feet were bound together and tied to the floor and so he could not adjust his stance to give him a more stable position. There was no relief from the pain in his arms and his legs. His thighs were burning from lack of movement over a long period of time. How long, he didn't know. He felt his eyelids closing and shook his head to stay awake showering more sweat droplets to the ground. His eyelids were so heavy and he wanted to sleep more than he had ever wanted to sleep before.

The chain jerked and Erik regained consciousness.

"Fuck!!" Erik spat on to the floor. He was hungry and thirsty. At regular intervals a young man would come into the room and give him water to drink through a water bottle and a tube. The man would bring the bottle up to his mouth and insert the tube into his lips. But it had been hours since the last water break and his mouth was dry. He licked his lips and they felt cracked and hard. His eyelids were so heavy and they closed even as he was thinking about the water. At that moment the door opened and Erik lifted his head. To his amazement it was Ceri who came into the room. Against all of the odds she had survived. She ran towards him and held his face in her hands.

"Quickly, get me out of this," said Erik.

Ceri seemed to panic and looked around the room anxiously, searching for a key. The room was bare and there was no sign of anything; no cupboards or desks, no hooks on the wall, just the chains that reached up towards the ceiling.

"Do you know here the key is?" she asked.

Eric shook his head. He wondered how Ceri had found him. He was too tired and confused to work it out.

"I'll need to look into the next room. I'll be quick," she said.

Ceri turned and opened the door. As she did so, a drone was entering the room. A red light flashed across its face and it raised its arm. Even as Ceri screamed the laser tore through her body. The drone swept his arm across and up and down and the laser cut through Ceri's body like a knife through butter. The smell of burning flesh filled the room and Ceri fell to the floor where a pool of her blood was already collecting.

"No!"

The chain jerked and Erik regained consciousness.

He didn't know how much more of this he could take.

CHAPTER 17

They were sitting around a campfire deep in the forest. After their joyful reunion, Lilly had taken Amelia to their base camp where there were few home comforts, but which at least was a reasonable distance away from Kielder. During the walk, Amelia had recounted what had happened to her since that fateful day when they had last seen each other. Lilly had insisted that Amelia tell her everything, brushing aside her questions for now about where she had been, how she had found Amelia, and what the weapon was that took out the drones. When news of James and Jon was revealed, Lilly cried, but coped better than might be expected. She was expecting the worst and what she heard from Amelia was not exactly a huge shock to her. Her over-arching emotion was still one of relief at finding Amelia. The last thing that Amelia told her was about the scene in Sophie's office and how she had had to leave Erik.

"I need to go back there mum," she said. "I need to go back soon."

"I would say you can't go anywhere for a couple of weeks the state you are in," replied Lilly, "but maybe, after what you said about your condition – I still find it hard to believe – but even so, it's going to take a couple of days even for you. We might be able to do something about your leg but the break in your arm has to heal or you'll be no good to anyone."

"I know. But I don't think Erik is going to have long."

Lilly put her arm around Amelia's shoulders and gave her a squeeze. "It may be too late already. I'm sorry. If it is there is nothing we can do about it. But we have to believe that in a few days Erik will still be alive."

Amelia stared into the flames. It would be dawn in a few hours but meanwhile the forest was black, the canopy blocking out any light from the moon, and the flames flickered brightly, sending burning embers upwards, in spirals, like fireflies.

Amelia woke to see her mother's face. She was lying in a sleeping bag inside a tent and her mother was kneeling by her side.

"Where am I?"

"It's ok Amy. Just relax. You passed out last night. You've been through such a lot. You needed to sleep."

Amelia noticed that she arm had been placed in a sort of cast and there was no pain. She unzipped the sleeping bag and looked at her leg. There was a dressing applied and it was strapped tightly around her lower leg.

"Wait here. I'll get you some breakfast," said Lilly.

Breakfast was dry bread and fruit, with water. As she bit into an apple and chewed it, Amelia remembered the weapon that had taken out the two robots.

"What was that thing mum? The weapon."

"It was an electromagnetic pulse gun."

"And that does ... what? ... exactly?" From her school days, now a very long time ago, Amelia had a recollection that electromagnetic radiation was light. Had a light gun taken out those two machines?

"It fires an intense burst of radiation. It's enough to fry any electrical device within a radius of about fifty metres."

"Wow. How many of those things have you got? I need one." Amelia was not joking. With such a weapon she had a chance of getting at Sophie, and more importantly of rescuing Erik.

"Just the one, I'm afraid. And it was only charged for one shot."

The disappointment was written all over Amelia's face.

"Sorry Amy. The guys at Anglesey knew about the robots apparently and they gave me the EMP ..."

"The what?" Amelia interrupted.

"EMP – electromagnetic pulse. That's what they call it. Anyway, they gave me this one. But it took a huge amount of electricity to get it charged. There is no way we can recharge it out here in the field."

Amelia looked crestfallen but then remembered that she had not asked her mum yet about her story.

"Anyway, mum. I want to hear everything that happened to you. Right from that first day when you went on top on your own."

Lilly sighed. "Ok," she said, "but it's a long story."

CHAPTER 18

The next two days were two of the worst of Amelia's life and there had been some bad ones. She felt so guilty about Erik, who must have known that in causing a distraction to give Amelia the chance to make her escape, he was resigning himself to death, possibly a painful one, at the hands of Sophie. She had not been able to save her brother and despite her efforts she had not been able to save her father. She was determined to save Erik who, more than anyone, deserved to be saved. The truth was, however, that she had a broken arm and she needed to rest and give her body time to heal. The first day, after hearing her mother's story she slept deeply. The second day she was more agitated and spent time talking with Lilly about the options.

She was sitting outside with Lilly and two men who had been introduced to her. Peter Carr was an ex-soldier who was now the leader of the new regime in Anglesey. Sean Cassidy was a colleague of Erik's from the Anglesey City Guard who had some experience of Kielder, having accompanied Erik on a previous visit there. Lilly explained how she had found her way to Anglesey, seeking news of Amelia, having been told by Elizabeth and Jill, the friends of Amelia's that by coincidence had found her unconscious body, that she was alive and well.

"When I arrived at Anglesey I realised that I had just missed you," said Lilly. "Peter and Sean told me what you and Erik had set out to do and also that in their opinion there was very little chance of success."

"That would be effing no chance," said Sean dourly.

"And it would seem that we were right," added Peter. "I did tell Erik what I thought, that it was madness, and I think he didn't need telling to be honest ... but he was so keen to help you rescue your father."

This only made Amelia feel worse.

"It was when Lilly said she was intent on following you that we decided we needed to have a rethink," said Peter. "We wondered whether there was another way to look at the problem."

"Lateral thinking, lassie, that's what you call it. Lateral thinking," Sean said in his rough Scottish tones.

Amelia looked from Sean to Peter and back again, unsure what they were talking about.

"And that's when we thought about the BFG," said Sean.

"BFG?" Amelia shook her head slightly from side to side, her brow furrowed. "What was that?"

"BFG – big fucking gun ... pardon my French," said Sean.

"Oh," said Amelia suddenly realising.

"The electromagnetic pulse gun," said Peter. "We knew we only had a single shot but thought that if we could get to the complex and use it there we could knock out enough of the droids – all of those within range – that it would cause a big enough diversion to give our small task force a chance of getting in and getting you all out. It was a long shot but one that we thought was worth taking given what you and Erik did for us all."

"Thanks." Amelia was genuinely grateful for what they had been prepared to do. "But I still don't understand how you found me in the woods," she added.

"That," said Lilly, "was sheer coincidence. We were approaching the complex when we thought all hell had broken loose. We saw the lights and the copters. To be honest we thought that we had been spotted and we were preparing to defend ourselves when you came running down the hill towards us."

"And the rest is history," said Sean, smiling broadly.

"I'm glad you found me when you did," said Amelia, "but can we recharge the EM-thingy?"

Sean dipped his cup into the soup pot that was being heated between them and withdrew it, about half-full with a brownish thin liquid.

Peter sighed. "I'm afraid not," he said. "There is no way we can charge it out here in the field."

"So ... what's the plan?" Amelia looked at all three in turn.

Sean blew on the soup in his mug. "What do you think the biggest strength of Kielder is?"

Amelia didn't have to think about that very long at all. "The androids," she said, feeling a bit stupid to be stating the obvious. "I don't see how we have any chance of taking Kielder even if we could knock out half of the androids."

"Correct lassie. Now, what do you think their greatest weakness is?"

This was a much harder question. "I don't know ...," said Amelia. "Maybe ... No, I don't know."

"You dinnae think that it could be ... the androids?"

"What? What makes you say that? How can they be a weakness?"

Sean smiled enigmatically and looked at Peter, as if to ask, shall I tell her or would you like to?

"You said," Peter explained, "that we couldn't take Kielder even if we could knock out half of the androids."

"Yes," said Amelia, still not following.

"Well, what if we could knock all of them out?"

"Their biggest weakness," said Sean, "is that they are so reliant on the droids. Their conventional defences are weak."

"Besides, there would be so much confusion if they were all knocked out together that even their conventional defence would be ineffective." Peter grabbed a cup and helped himself to some of the soup. "It would take them time to sort themselves out, and during that time we could take advantage of the confusion." He sipped the soup and said, "Mmmm, that's nice."

"But I thought you said we can't charge the gun."

"We cannae do that," said Sean, "but there is another way."

CHAPTER 19

The announcement about the gene treatment at Kielder created great excitement amongst the elite who were offered the opportunity. The treatment was initially restricted to about three hundred of those in the upper echelons of the society and almost all were quick to take advantage. The laboratory was working around the clock to make the serum and then administer it. A small number of people chose not to have the treatment. These were generally those that were deeply religious or who had a particularly pessimistic vision of the future.

None of those treated, however, showed any side effects. It seemed that the benefits that Amelia obtained would probably be unique to her and were probably related to the fact that she was in hibernation for a quarter of a century after the therapy. Sophie was disappointed about this but at the end of the day she was prepared to play the long game. A life span of a thousand years was not to be sniffed and at, to all intents and purposes, she now considered herself to be immortal.

It was several days since Amelia's escape and Sophie spent an uncomfortable time in Mark Bailey's office explaining how she got away. It was embarrassing that a young girl had escaped from the office of the Chief of Security, especially given the presence of androids in the room. However, Bailey was more concerned about the reports of two destroyed androids. The two shells that had been recovered from the night-time pursuit of Amelia were wrecked. The electronics were fried. It would take months to repair them, if it was possible at all.

"So, what do you think did it?" Bailey asked.

"The guys in the lab are saying that only a huge burst of radiation could have done that."

"And that means?"

"Some sort of specialist weapon – one that can fry electronics."

Bailey looked concerned. He started to imagine what that sort of weapon could do to their defence system.

"How do you think the girl got hold of something like that?"

"We think it's unlikely she had it. If she had it then she would have most likely brought it with her in the first place."

Bailey nodded.

We think ...," Sophie continued, "that she had assistance. There were a few weapons like that at Anglesey. They were mothballed. To be honest, I didn't even know they were still working."

Bailey's eyes widened. "They? How many?"

"Very few ... Three. Four at most. And not all of those would necessarily still be operational."

Sophie didn't seem totally convincing.

Bailey let out a deep sigh and clasped his hands together in front of him on his desk. "So, what's your plan of action?"

"We've doubled the perimeter patrols and we have helicopters in the sky almost every hour."

Bailey still looked concerned. During the last quarter of a century there had been attacks on the base. But nothing for the last fifteen years and that was longer than he had been in charge. he was acutely aware that they had limited combat experience and what had happened at Anglesey was playing on his mind. Was there a chance that Kielder was going to come under attack?

"What about that Erik chap? What have you got out of him so far?"

"He doesn't know much. He is at breaking point. The only thing he told us was that they had stopped off at Haltwhistle. I already knew that. I have a couple of informants there. So his story tallies with what we know. I don't think he is going to tell us much more."

Sophie took the elevator down to the dungeon. It was true what she had told Bailey. She was convinced that Erik knew nothing more than he had told them. He could tell her nothing about the weapon that had been used and as far as she was concerned he was of no further use to them. That was her professional opinion of course. She liked to mix business and pleasure and thought that another session with Erik would be good for her – she needed de-stressing. Besides she had a few toys she had not tried yet.

CHAPTER 20

"You see, the key to taking out the androids is to take out their power supply," said Sean Cassidy. "The complex gets almost all of its electricity from the hydro-electric power station. They have a small emergency supply to keep the hospitals going and the other essential services ... but the androids require loads of power on a regular basis. Take out the power station and you take out the androids."

"Where is the station?" Amelia was interested.

"On the east of the water, where the reservoir naturally empties in the North Tyne river. There's something called a Francis Turbine, nine hundred kilowatts per hour are generated on a continual basis. There used to be a larger turbine that operated on water release but that has not operated for years. The smaller turbine is sufficient for their needs anyway, whereas the larger system used to provide power to all the people in and around Newcastle."

"So how do we get there and how to we take it out?"

Sean looked at Peter who nodded, as if to give him permission to continue.

"That, lassie, is the difficult part. The plant is strongly protected. There are four or five of the androids outside at all times. They know that the power station is a weak point for them and it is protected around the clock. There is no way we can storm it and ..."

"But there must be a way," interrupted Amelia.

"Aye, there is a way, but it is potentially fatal. Only someone with superhuman strength could pull it off."

"Go on."

It was Peter who continued, "We think, probably, that the only way to take it out is to enter the way the water does, from the reservoir."

"Doesn't that go straight to the turbines?" Lilly was worried.

Peter explained the plan, with occasional clarification from Sean, who was an engineer. Amelia would have to swim in the lake towards the point where the water left to form the river North Tyne. She would need to swim underwater and negotiate several filters and grills that the water flowed through to protect the turbines from debris in the water. Finally, she would be able to approach the turbines and this was the most dangerous moment because the water would flow down into the turbines with a force that could suck her into the machinery. Sean drew a diagram and explained where she would have to place a small explosive charge so that it would have the greatest effect. The drones operated for about twelve hours before needing to be recharged. That meant that about twelve hours after the detonation all the drones would be dead. It was a small window of opportunity. Sean estimated that they might be able to repair the damage in about ten hours but more likely it would be nearer twenty hours. There was probably going to be about six to ten hours, at least, where the base would be unprotected by the drones. That was the opportunity. It was their only opportunity.

"What happens if I succeed?"

"The base is considerably easier to attack than Anglesey. There are several points of attack including across the lake, and the forest provides considerable cover," said Peter.

Sean was laying a map onto the ground in front of them. "We are dependent upon some local support. We've been in touch with the Haltwhistle group you told us about. They weren't keen at first, to be honest, but I think we can rely upon them."

Amelia was alarmed. "Please get a message to the leader there, a guy called Ethan. They have a spy. Liam. An ugly runt of a man. He betrayed us to Sophie. We can't be sure there are not more spies. It's important Ethan understands this and ..."

"Dinnae worry lass. He already understands the sensitivity of the situation. Even if news of an attack leaks out, they will not know what our plan is."

"Nevertheless," said Peter, "might be worth double-checking with Ethan that he knows that his group is compromised."

"Aye, you're right. I'll sort that out straight away."

CHAPTER 21

In three days Amelia had healed in a way that her mother found extraordinary given that she had never seen anything like it before. It was one thing to be told about something incredible but quite another to see it with your own eyes. They were close to the lake shore – Peter, Amelia and Lilly – and waiting for cover of darkness to hide Amelia's entry to the lake.

Amelia and Lilly had spoken in depth about what had happened in the bunker. Neither could provide much insight about why Amelia's father had pretended to be dead. It wasn't clear what he had intended to achieve. They thought it likely that he was trying to protect them but it was hard to work out how he thought that what he did was the best option. Nevertheless, neither thought badly of him. They both were aware that it was only thanks to him that they were alive at all and they also respected his decision not to throw his lot in with the government and aristocracy. He had been a good man and they were still both proud of him. But Amelia still had some questions.

"You're absolutely sure, mum, that dad didn't treat you too?" She had asked this before but she still had her doubts.

"As sure as I can be. Certainly I don't have any special powers like you do. God, I wish I had done and I could have given those bastards in Chester what they deserved."

"But you don't think that you have longevity without the extra abilities?"

"It's possible Amelia. I suppose it is. Time will tell, eh? But I don't think so."

Amelia looked a bit puzzled and so Lilly continued, "Jon and I did speak about this. I didn't know that he had perfected the treatment – honestly I didn't. But we did talk about what we would want in the future and I told him several times that I didn't want to live an unnaturally long life."

Lilly looked at the sky. It was darkening but it would still be better to wait for a while. "There's an old story – The

Immortals, I think it's called – about people who live forever. The idea is that if you live forever, then you will do almost everything that you could do. You'll be an engineer, a scientist, an artist, a whore, a queen, a tramp – you'll achieve everything, but also there'll be times, aeons, when you do nothing at all, when you live quite a boring life. Because forever is a very long time."

"And that's bad? I wouldn't mind a brief spell as a queen." Amelia was surprised she was still able to keep her sense of humour in the circumstances.

"Well, the thing is, however unlikely some of these scenarios are, given long enough, they will happen. Since we will be everything then in some sense we will be nothing and nobody. Life would cease to have meaning. Infinite time would wipe out the identity of individuals. This leads to the idea that far from fearing death we should embrace it; since without death our lives would become meaningless."

"Wow – that's a bit dark."

Lilly put her arm around Amelia. She hadn't meant to disturb her. "I suppose it is. And I'm sure you will have plenty of fantastic experiences. I just thought it wasn't for me. Your dad knew that." And she gave her daughter a kiss on the head.

The night closed in and they were lucky. It was a cloudy night and there was no starlight. Even the moon was not visible. They crept towards the edge of the forest and Peter made sure that Amelia was clear about everything that she needed to do. The darkness sprawled over the lake and hung heavy around them, claustrophobic and threatening. Amelia and Lilly hugged; a close and tight hug of ones who knew they may never meet again. Lilly didn't want Amelia to go. It was cruel that after all those weeks, months even, of pain and worry, with only the hope of seeing her children again to keep her going, their reconciliation could be so brief. But she understood that Amelia had to go. That she had to do this.

Amelia stepped into the water wearing shorts and a t-shirt and with a water-proof rucksack attacked to her back. Without delay, knowing that every second out of the water was an opportunity to be spotted, she slipped quietly into the water so that within no time only her head was visible. She looked back, once, and saw Peter standing with his arm around her mother. Even from a distance, and with a momentary glance, she could see the tears in her mother's eyes. She swam out into the lake and tried to focus on her objectives – but one idea clung to her mind and refused to leave – *it is only that we die that makes life bearable at all.*

CHAPTER 22

As she approached the power station she tried to keep her body underwater at all times, bringing her head to the surface for air only when absolutely necessary, and then only for the shortest time. Being spotted as she approached the station, and being taken out by a sniper, was one of the greatest risks. Eventually, she followed the water into a dimly lit tunnel and ahead of her she could see the first of the barriers that she was expecting. She was carried along by the water towards the barrier and then pushed against the metal. Clinging to the aluminium bars, she took the opportunity to check for guards. She knew that she needed to be quiet despite there being nobody in immediate view. There was an eerie feeling of movement in the tunnel brought on by the sound of the water slapping against the sides of the tunnel and the shimmering reflections of the waves on the ceiling. There was also the drone of the turbines, amplified by the shape of the tunnel so that it sounded to Amelia like the low groan of an animal in pain. Strapped to her waist she had a pair of metal cutters and she unclipped these now. The plan was to use these to make a hole in the barrier that was large enough to slip through. As instructed by Peter, she used the metal cutter under water, so that the noise of breaking metal would be absorbed by the mass of water. There was a tow path on either side of the water, inside the tunnel, but it was also blocked by gates and attempting to break these would create more noise. She would also be more exposed and, besides, according to Peter they could not rule out the possibility that there were motion detectors focussed on the tow path.

Given her strength she found the metal relatively easy to break with the cutters and within about fifteen minutes she had created a space she could fit through. She reattached the cutters to her waist and ducked under the water, before guiding herself through the hole that she had created. She moved forwards, keeping close to the left-hand tow path and with as little of her head out of the water as possible; just her eyes and occasionally

102

her nose to breath. The weight of the water was now pushing her forwards with greater force as the channel narrowed and it was with some difficulty that she was able to keep her movement forward slow enough that she felt in control. Twenty feet further on and she reached the second barrier. This was a mesh. It was probably too fine to get the cutters into and climbing over the top was the only option. However, it was not high, protruding just a few inches above the surface of the water, and she took time to check that nobody was around. She spent nearly ten minutes just watching, until she was convinced that there was nobody. She pulled herself upwards out of the water, effortlessly, and slipped as quietly as possible into the water on the other side. She held on to the mesh and felt her legs pulled out from under her towards the turbine. The tow path had been sloping upwards so that the water level was now at least five feet below the level of the path – there was no way to climb out of the water here and going forward to the turbines was the only available route. At least the sound from the rotating turbines, much louder now as it filled the confined space of the tunnel, would mask any sound that she made.

When she was ready, she let herself go and her body rushed forwards towards the turbines. She had spotted a ladder that was built into the wall and led up from the surface of the water to the tow path and that was her goal. At first she had thought that she could somehow hold onto the wall. However, it was slippery, covered in a green slime, and there was nothing to hold on to. For a few seconds she started to panic as she realised that she was now out of control. She was hurtling forwards towards the turbines and certain death. Quickly, she composed herself and started to swim against the flow and a little towards the wall. It was now that she realised why it had to be her who took this part of the mission on. Anyone else would have been unable to control themselves and would be sucked underwater at the turbines to have their bodies chewed up and mangled by the machinery. If this had happened it could have temporarily stopped the energy supply but at the cost of her life. She was not prepared for that deal. It took all of her strength and power but she was able to maintain her position close to the wall, even though she was slipping inexorably towards the turbines. With a supreme effort, as she passed the ladder she managed to grab hold of a rung and cling to it, pulling the rest of her body into the wall. Her feet found the rungs underwater which was a moment of relief.

Before pulling herself out of the water she spent a few moments going through in her head what Peter and Sean had told her. When she made her move, she wanted to be able to move fast and decisively so as to minimise the chance of being discovered. When she had thought through the plan several times she pulled herself up out of the black water and onto the path. Ahead, as expected, she could see a control room. She crept towards it, keeping in the shadows by the wall, until she could see clearly the control room, which was quite well lit, and could identify that there were three people inside; two men and a woman. They didn't look to be armed. She placed her hand on the door handle and gave it a quick turn. It was moving. The door was not locked. She pulled out the knife that was strapped to her leg and readied herself. She didn't like violence, but what she was about to do was necessary to save Erik and get to Sophie.

CHAPTER 23

Sophie was just about to go to bed when the lights went off in her bedroom as a sound, like thunder, rocked the air. She walked outside of her apartment and noticed that the lights were also off in the communal corridors. She went back to her apartment and located a candle that she had stored in a drawer for this eventuality and lit it using a flint set which she always kept in the drawer. Under the flickering warm light she got dressed and made her way to her office to find the place was awash with people. It was evident that there was a major issue. There was some emergency lighting around the complex but it was obvious that the main grid was down. She realised that she needed to go to the power station which was just over a mile away.

Downstairs, she instructed one of the androids to accompany her and took one of the electric cars, making sure that she chose one that was fully charged. The android sat in the back of the truck and afforded her some protection. She was leaving the immediate vicinity of the camp and that meant that there was a chance that she could be attacked. It had crossed her mind, of course, that this was not a technical fault or an accident but was in fact part of a concerted attack. As she drove down the stony road, dense forest on her left and the dark still surface of the lake on her right, she started to think that an attack was the most likely explanation. It was too much of a coincidence that this had happened given the incident with Amelia Savage a few days ago.

Even before she arrived at the power station it was obvious that her suspicion was correct. There were interruptions to the power supply from time to time of course. But the evidence of an explosion was all around and by the time she pulled into the small gravelled car park, the place was teeming with people. A line of men snaking from the lakeside to the power station were transporting buckets of water from hand to hand. The fire was under control but dense smoke was still billowing upwards in the darkness.

The workers inside the control room had barely had a chance to understand what was happening. One of the men, furthest from the door, had heard a noise and turned. By the time he had turned, he saw his colleague collapsing to the ground and was aware that there was a fourth person in the room. He saw a knife, the spurt of blood, and his female colleague collapsed to the floor holding her throat, as blood pulsed out between her fingers. By the time the assailant was close to him he had had time to understand that there was a threat and to ready himself. However, she moved so quickly and with such purpose. In addition, she was armed and trained in combat and he was neither of these things. He only had time to put his arms up to protect himself before he was aware of pain in his stomach and looked down to see the knife withdrawing and blood gushing onto the floor of the control room. Within less than forty seconds of entering the room, Amelia had disabled or killed all three occupants and set about unpacking her backpack. Wrapped within a second layer of waterproof material was a small explosive device. She located the specific control boxes that Sean had described and placed the explosive into position. She lit the charge and retreated from the room. She ran down the tow path until she was out of danger from the explosion and pressed her back against the wall to wait. About ten seconds later there was a simultaneous explosion of sound and light as splinters of wood and glass were blown out of the control room.

It dawned on Sophie that the thunder she had heard had been the explosion. She brushed aside guards who tried to keep her out of the building for her own safety until she could see into the control room. Two corpses had already been dragged out and laid out in the corridor. Her assistant, Jacob Scott, was already on the scene and she asked him for an update.

"They were taken out before the explosion," he said.

"How long are we looking at?"

"According to the chief engineer, Reuben, the power's going to be off all night and probably most of tomorrow."

Sophie instantly understood the implications of what Jacob we telling her. As Head of Security she understood all too well that by the morning the androids would be running out of power.

"Tell them they have to get it back online by first light – understood?"

Jacob nodded but did not look confident that his boss's instructions would be able to be complied with.

Meanwhile, Sophie marched back to her car, where the android was patiently waiting. She needed to get back to the camp to prepare for the worst.

CHAPTER 24

The drones were designed to automatically return to the research block when their power became low. The power threshold that triggered the point of return depended upon how far the drone was away from the charging point to ensure that they could always make it back before running out of power and being left high and dry. By mid-morning almost all of the drones were motionless, standing in their charging bays in the basement of the research facility. The bay was dimly illuminated by emergency lighting, but the charging bays, that were placed along both sides of the long basement, were quiet and lifeless. The drones stood like corpses waiting for the spark of electricity to bring them to life, like Frankenstein's monster. Even when the electricity was restored a full charge would take at least five hours. Normally, the drones were rotated so that at any time there were some on charge. However, when the power went out yesterday evening the numbers in the charging bay had quickly swelled, as drones returned to the bays and waited patiently, a residual charge allowing minimal operation. Even the drones that had a full charge at the time of the power outage were now returning to the bay. This left Kielder Water defenceless.

Actually, it was not true that they were defenceless. There was a small military police operation and they were well armed. It was more than a decade since they had experienced any combat though and their reliance on the drones for frontline operations had left them short of experience and confidence. Rumours that the power cut was the result of hostile activity spread like wildfire and combined with the gossip about Amelia's escape from the window of Sophie Wassell's office was causing panic to infect the residents and police alike like a contagion. The fate of Anglesey, something that had been long-discussed in the coffee shops and restaurants frequented by the elite, was foremost in their minds so that by the time that the attackers arrived in the camp resistance was fragile.

The attack was orchestrated by Peter Carr who had used the helicopters to shuttle as many men as possible from Anglesey to within a four-hour march to Kielder Water. Nevertheless, they would have been undermanned to say the least if he had not been able to persuade Ethan to mobilise the Haltwhistle community. As dawn had approached, Sophie had positioned forty of the militia to defend the power station, expecting that it could come under further attack. She was right. The Haltwhistle group were several hundred strong and approached the camp from the south, taking the power station on their way. There was fierce fighting and the defenders held out for nearly an hour before deserting their posts and fleeing towards the illusion of safety at the main base. The Haltwhistle force followed them so that there was bedlam as the two forces flooded into the camp at about the same time, leaving the defenders who had dug in facing south with the difficult decision about who was friend and who was foe. Just as the situation could hardly become more confusing, Peter Carr drove the Kielder Water force into the camp from the north catching the defenders in a pincer movement. Casualties mounted on both sides but it was evident that the defenders were losing ground quickly and in danger of being over-run.

Meanwhile the drones, which would have almost certainly been able to defeat the invaders had they been operational, lay still in the charging bays, oblivious to the chaos developing above them.

CHAPTER 25

Under cover of darkness Amelia had crept into the camp and found her way onto the roof of the research facility via a fire escape. Over several hours she had worked her way deeper into the facility until she was close to where she believed Eric would be being held. There she waited, secreted in a store room behind a wall of boxes, until she heard the sound of fighting in the camp. She knew that if she moved too early then the chances of getting out safely with Erik were small. However, once the fighting started there would be so many distractions that the odds would become stacked on her side. She found waiting difficult though. Had she and Erik not been delayed at Haltwhistle would they have arrived in time to save her father? She had no idea whether Erik was still alive but she believed that with every hour that passed the chances that he was dead increased.

She became aware of shouting and increased movement outside the store room and shortly afterwards the sounds of gunfire rang out. Within a few minutes it was evident that a large-scale assault had begun and this, she knew, was her moment. She put her ear to the door and when it seemed quiet in the corridor outside she cautiously opened the door and left the store room. She was not entirely certain which way to go and it took her a while to find herself in the lower levels of the research building where she hoped to find Erik. At one point she entered a foyer and was confronted by two men and a woman coming the other way. Her heart missed a beat and she steeled herself for confrontation. Unless they were armed she would be confident of taking them out and she expected to have to do so – she was hardly dressed inconspicuously since her clothes were dirty and tattered from her activities in the power station. However, the three barely gave her a second glance. They clearly had other things on their mind and were engrossed in conversation as they slipped through the door through which Amelia had just entered.

From the foyer Amelia found an open stairwell and descended below ground level. It was clear that she was in a medical facility and looking through the circular window of one door she saw a ward with half-a-dozen beds, most occupied with patients. Down here, in the relatively stark and clinical environment of what was obviously a hospital she felt her appearance was even more out of place and was sure that she would be challenged if she was encountered. On the other hand, there was less chance of there being armed personnel down here and so her confidence was high.

When she felt she had exhausted the search on this floor she returned to the stairwell and went down to the next floor. It was dark below and she half expected lights to come on automatically but they did not. Perhaps there was no power on this floor. She walked slowly with her hand outstretched on her right, feeling the wall as she walked along, allowing her eyes to slowly become accustomed to the low light levels. A little light found its way down the stairwell and infused the whole area below. At first it had been black but now she found that she was able to see reasonably well.

She came to one door, on the right, and it was locked with an old-fashioned bar that she was able to lift up. Inside the room it was dark, pitch black. She opened the door wider to allow what little light there was in the corridor to reach the room. She reached out with her hands trying to feel her way around the room. As she started to see shapes she thought she saw a bed in front of her and then she shrieked as she felt a hand grab hers. The shock of the contact made her step backwards. But quickly it dawned on her that this was someone in a bed, possibly ill, maybe captive, but certainly not a threat. She ventured forward again.

"Who's there?" she asked.

CHAPTER 26

"Jim," a dry voice croaked softly.

"And Helen." This was a different voice, further to the left.

There were two patients in the room, being held captive. Each was handcuffed to the metal bed frame but they were able to tell Amelia that the key to the handcuffs was on a hook by the door. Despite the gloom, Amelia retrieved this and was able to free them from their restraints.

"That's better," said Jim. He rubbed the wrist on his right hand, the one that had been cuffed, with his other hand.

"Do you know if there are any others being held down here?" asked Amelia.

Jim had managed to lower the metal bar on the side of his bed and was sitting up with his feet on the floor. "There are some dreadful sounds that we sometimes hear. There's at least one other person down here."

"Down the corridor," said the woman, Helen. She was looking for clothes. Like Jim she was almost naked and she needed to find something to wear if she was to get out of here. "Who are you? What's happened here?"

"The camp is being attacked," explained Amelia. "You have a chance to get away. You need to move quickly."

Amelia had no time to help them. She had done all that she could. As she slipped back into the corridor she paused at the door, looking back, and whispered softly, "Good luck." Then she continued down to the next door on the right, which was also locked.

She lifted the bar which was identical to the one on the previous door and slowly opened the door. It swung inwards and revealed another dark room. As she did so, she heard loud voices behind her. She looked back and saw two guards with torches who were peering into the previous room and speaking with Helen and Jim. One of the guards was already in the room – the other was just outside the doorway. Amelia rushed back and as she approached the first guard he turned. His flashlight blinded Amelia momentarily and she felt something hard make a glancing blow to her head. She managed to reach out and grab the guard's arm – the one that was holding a long baton – and she pulled him with such force that he flew across the corridor like a rag doll and crashed into the wall on the other side, crumpling to the ground.

Amelia grabbed the second guard by his lapels and lifted him off the ground to his surprise. Before he had time to speak she hurled him at the opposite wall. He fell to the ground and was on one knee starting to get up when she kicked him in the head and he fell to the ground and lay still.

Back in the second room Amelia asked if anyone was there. There was no reply.

As she moved into the room she was aware of something in front of her and she stretched out her arms to feel it. Her fingers made contact and it became immediately apparent it was a person. She ran back outside and found one of the torches that was on the floor near to the first guard that she had incapacitated. Returning to the room she used the torch to illuminate the body that was in the middle of the room.

It was Erik. He was unconscious, hopefully not dead. But Amelia saw with horror that he was painfully thin and his naked body that hung suspended from the ceiling was bruised and sore with dried blood in a great many places.

It took her some time to remove the chains that were restraining Erik and by the time she had done so he was responding, groggily as if drugged. But he was alive and that was the main thing. She lifted his body onto the shoulders and carried him out of the room and up the stairs. This would have been easy for her before, but now that his body weighed so little it was effortless.

As she reached the top of the stairs at ground level her eyes struggled momentarily to adapt to the brighter light levels. She froze as she sensed the presence of someone else just before she saw the unmistakable form of Sophie Wassell. Sophie was not alone. Next to her was a droid and it was evidently charged and fully operational.

"How ...?" Amelia began, as she lowered Erik to the floor.

"How come I am protected by my ... friend?" said Sophie, patting the metal form next to her. "You don't think I am that stupid. You have succeeded in disabling our defences and ... anyway, Kielder Water will probably fall. But I would not leave myself so vulnerable. My friend here has access to a charging bay in my office, which has an emergency power supply. It may not save the camp, but it will deal with you – and that," said Sophie gesturing in the direction of Erik's body on the floor, "and enable me to escape again."

Amelia was speechless. After all that she had been through, was it to end this way? Here? Like this?

"I have too many years to look forward to for me to let you stop me," said Sophie.

At that moment the doors swung open at the end of the foyer and Jim and Helen stepped in. They were lost and still trying to find their way out. They stopped in their tracks as the door swung closed behind them.

"Kill those two," commanded Sophie.

The droid turned towards the pair and raised its arm. A red laser shot forwards and ripped through Jim and Helen's bodies barely before they had time to realise what was happening.

Amelia was horrified but also was kicking herself. That – whilst the android was killing Jim and Helen – was perhaps the one chance she had to attack the drone. It had been momentarily distracted and that might have given her an extra second or two to race across the room and engage it before it fired at her. She regretted that she had not realised the opportunity and that Jim and Helen had now died for no reason.

"Now," said Sophie, smirking and looking Amelia in the eye, "kill those two," as she pointed towards Amelia and Erik.

CHAPTER 27

It seemed it really was going to end here ... this way. Amelia felt strangely calm as she waited for the end. At least she had found Erik. And even though she could not save him, it was better for her to die now with him, that to live an eternity without him. She started to close her eyes ... waiting ... when she sensed something on her left.

The swing doors on the left flew open and Lilly came rushing through them. She was holding a semi-automatic machine-gun and she sprayed bullets towards Sophie and the droid. Sophie threw herself to the floor and the android turned towards the source of the bullets that were striking its body but seemingly causing no damage. In the 20th century the science-fiction writer Asimov had postulated three laws of robotics that future robots should obey. The first law was that a robot may not injure a human being or, through inaction, allow a human being to come to harm. It was obvious that this law had not been part of its makers' thinking. The second law was that a robot must obey the orders given to it by human beings, except where such orders would conflict with the first Law. The third law was that a robot must protect its own existence as long as such protection does not conflict with the first or second Laws. The second and third laws had been built in to the software that drove the machines. The robots would attempt to protect themselves. In this case, the software came to the conclusion that it should deal with the threat that had just appeared before returning to complete Sophie's instructions.

The droid was not conscious of course. It had no understanding in the true sense of the word and could experience no emotion. It was a machine – nothing more and nothing less. It merely behaved as though it was conscious, as though it could understand. However, it was an efficient and an effective machine and it obliterated Lilly's body as she rushed towards it using its laser fire power.

Amelia would later run through this scenario in her head over and over again and wonder whether she could have done more, whether anything could have been done to save her mother's life. But at that moment she behaved as a machine herself. Whether it was because of what had just happened with Helen and Jim, where she had not taken the opportunity; perhaps her brain was now primed to behave in this way ... or whether she would have always behaved in this way, she would never know. The important thing was that she did act with machine-like efficiency. She also moved with super-human speed. It was a speed that the android was not programmed to anticipate in a human and because of that – and because of the distraction of the woman bursting in with the machine gun – it was unable to react in time to prevent Amelia from reaching it. Amelia hit her metal opponent with speed and considerable force and she knocked it to the ground. As they fell, together, the robot beneath her, she grabbed the head of the droid and smashed it down on the floor. The robot grabbed her and tried to push her away. Probably it was programmed to avoid close combat where at all possible since at greater separation its superior speed and weaponry would give it a greater edge. However, Amelia was stronger than any human opponent it had faced in the past and it was unable to break her grip on its head. It was not clear to Amelia whether hitting the head on the floor was having any effect. At the back of her mind was the concern that the robot still had a laser weapon and although it would be risky for it to use it in close combat – because it could injure itself – sooner or later it might come to the conclusion that it was a risk worth taking. The robot was still horizontal on the floor. Amelia brought her feet up to place them on the shoulders of the android and threw herself forwards, over the robots head, still keeping tight hold of the head. At the right moment, she pulled with all her might on the head, pulling it upwards away from its body, whilst simultaneously pushing down with her legs on its shoulders. With super-human strength, that surprised even her, she pulled the head away and it broke from the body, causing her to fall further forwards and away from the android. The head remained in Amelia's hands and was lifeless. The body made occasional twitching movements but was obviously no longer a threat.

CHAPTER 28

Amelia's first thought when she realised she had defeated the robot was a simple one – retribution. She immediately sought out Sophie but saw that she was no longer in the room. She had escaped Lilly's bullets or, if she had been hit then it had not been fatal.

The roof. It was obvious that Sophie would seek out the helicopters again as a way of making an escape. Amelia could not let her get away with it a second time.

She raced up the stairs until she reached the top and burst through a door that led on to the roof. She looked left where there was nothing much. To the right, about thirty yards away, was a heliport and several helicopters were parked nearby. She sprinted towards them and saw that one of the helicopter's blades were starting to spin. The helicopter juddered slightly as it started to rise. She could just see Sophie in the cockpit. It was like the situation in Anglesey except that this time Sophie was on her own. Amelia was surprised that she seemed capable of flying the craft but it was obvious that she had some ability as the helicopter was rising.

If Amelia did not have exceptional speed it is unlikely that she would have made it. As it was she sprinted to the take-off point and arrived there as the helicopter was swiftly rising. She jumped forward and upwards and caught the rail at the bottom of the helicopter as it accelerated upwards.

The helicopter rotated and was about to move away from the roof when Amelia was able to pull herself upwards and on to the rail from where she could access the cockpit. Sophie was startled to see that Amelia was on-board and pushed the throttle to accelerate the craft. Within seconds Amelia was inside the cockpit and was grappling with Sophie. The helicopter was moving rapidly out over the lake but was starting to lose ground. About a hundred yards across the lake it struck the water and as it started to sink Amelia pushed Sophie out of the cockpit door so that they

118

both fell out into the water. The helicopter started to sink as the blades stopped spinning.

Amelia and Sophie were both under the water. Amelia grabbed Sophie's throat and started to squeeze. Sophie's hands flapped and tried to pull Amelia's arms away but of course with no effect – Amelia was far too strong. With a kick of her legs, Amelia pushed down on Sophie's neck so that she could momentarily take a huge lungful of air before submerging again. Sophie's eyes were wide with panic and Amelia stared at her, making eye contact on purpose, and watching as the strength and life seeped out of her.

Eventually Sophie's body went limp and her arms stopped scrabbling towards Amelia. Her mouth opened loosely and her eyes remained open, staring still, but with no meaning. Amelia burst to the top and took another gasp of air before returning below. She continued to hold on to Sophie and to squeeze the throat of the woman who had killed both of her parents in cold blood. She also thought about what Erik had been through. She wanted to leave no possibility that Sophie could survive. It was better to be absolutely sure than to allow the smallest possibility that she could survive. Grabbing hold of Sophie's lifeless body she swam to the shore and lay panting in the shallow water. She committed two further acts. The first was to get hold of Sophie's head and force it backwards until the neck snapped, leaving the head hanging at a grotesque angle. Now she was satisfied that she was dead. The second was to grab the bone amulet that was hanging around the broken neck and pull it. The chain snapped and Amelia clasped the small piece of bone in her hand tightly; the only piece of her father that remained.

Suddenly she remembered Erik and rushed back towards the research building whilst the sounds of gunfire still echoed around in the grey morning.

CHAPTER 29

Kielder Water fell, just as Anglesey had fallen, although this time there were no escapees. Only those who surrendered survived but their numbers were quite great. There was no leadership in the defending forces – in stark contrast that exhibited by Peter Carr and Ethan – and once it became apparent that the camp was being overrun the defenders capitulated with little resistance.

Amelia found Erik, still barely conscious but alive. She also found her mother's remains. Later she would take them and bury them in the forest. Although Erik offered to help she went on her own and dug a deep pit in an area of the forest that was far from any path. After she lowered her mother into the hole she was just about to start covering her with earth when she remembered her father's bone. She felt in her pocket and brought out the small ivory-coloured piece. She kissed it and then dropped it into the pit before covering the remains with earth.

She didn't mark the grave. In the future there would be nobody to know and nobody to care. But she would know – and she would care – and she would remember. And that is all that mattered.

CHAPTER 30

The surf crashed onto the rocks below and seagulls called out, gliding across the blue sky. Amelia and Erik lay on the bed enjoying a quiet morning, listening to the sounds of the sea and the noises from the city waking up around them. It had been six months since the fall of Kielder Water and life had returned to normal at Anglesey. Except that there was nothing normal about life at all and certainly it was a time of great change. The rate at which trade was growing was extraordinary and little by little, bit by bit, normality was returning in the sense that people started to become more concerned with the everyday trivia that used to occupy people's thoughts, before survival became the over-riding obsession. Every day brought some new innovation or brought some old technology or idea back. But things would never be truly normal again.

For Amelia and Erik life was idyllic. The past had been horrific but the present was what mattered. The future also mattered, but Amelia did not want to think much about that because she knew that she – a transhuman – would live for a thousand years, possibly much more if Sophie's view about the technological singularity was to come to fruition, whereas Erik was merely human and would live another forty or fifty years at best. Whenever Amelia thought about the future the image of Erik on his deathbed, whilst she – still a young girl – tended to him, haunted her. So she tried not to think about it. And yet, she knew that soon she would need to confront the future, especially because of the news that she had shared with Erik last week. She was pregnant. The first child who's parent would live to be a thousand years old would soon be born.

About the Author

Stephen Westland was born in Staffordshire in the UK. He has worked for most of his life as an academic and holds a Professorship at a leading British university. He is an independent writer and *Mutation*, the first book in The Millennium Girl series, is his first novel and was published in 2014. *Retribution*, the second book in the series, was published in 2015. He has also written short stories in several anthologies including *Murderous Tales* and *The Envelope*, both of which he co-edited.

Mutation
The Millennium Girl Series Book 1

Stephen Westland

Amelia Savage is a 17 year-old girl who is one of the lucky few that survived the great plague that wiped out ninety-nine per cent of the human population in 2022. Separated from her family she emerges from her bunker to find a world that is changed beyond her imaginings; a post-apocalyptic landscape dominated by a dystopian government elite and inhabited by brutal scavengers. Then she discovers that she is unique in the world and has unusual powers. Can she survive the warring factions and find her family before she is captured and used by the elite in their quest to achieve a transhuman state.

A Personal Message

I hope you enjoyed this book as much as I enjoyed writing it. As you might know by now it is part of a series about Amelia Savage, the first girl to live for 1000 years, the Millennium Girl.

If you are interested in some of the issues raised in this book such as gene therapy, transhumanism and immortality please visit the blog, http://millenniumgirlseries.wordpress.com/, which I set up to support this series of books.

Engaging with readers and hearing what they think is important to me. If you want to tell me what you think about the book please email me at stephenwestland@gmx.com. However, it is a tough world for independent writers like me and we need all of the help we can to be successful. So if you enjoyed the book please tell your friends about it and, if you can spare the time, please take a few minutes to enter a review about the book on Amazon. Positive reviews are so important to me.

Stephen Westland
7th January 2015

Printed in Great Britain
by Amazon.co.uk, Ltd.,
Marston Gate.